ENRICHED
KNIGHTS OF 4 BRETHREN

I0694464

Books by Jody Hedlund

Knights of Brethren Series
Enamored
Entwined
Ensnared
Enriched

The Fairest Maidens Series
Beholden
Beguiled
Besotted

The Lost Princesses Series
Always: Prequel Novella
Evermore
Foremost
Hereafter

Noble Knights Series
The Vow: Prequel Novella
An Uncertain Choice
A Daring Sacrifice
For Love & Honor
A Loyal Heart
A Worthy Rebel

Waters of Time Series
Come Back to Me
Never Leave Me

The Colorado Cowboys
A Cowboy for Keeps
The Heart of a Cowboy
To Tame a Cowboy

The Bride Ships Series
A Reluctant Bride
The Runaway Bride
A Bride of Convenience
Almost a Bride

The Orphan Train Series
An Awakened Heart: A Novella
With You Always
Together Forever
Searching for You

The Beacons of Hope Series
Out of the Storm: A Novella
Love Unexpected
Hearts Made Whole
Undaunted Hope
Forever Safe
Never Forget

The Hearts of Faith Collection
The Preacher's Bride
The Doctor's Lady
Rebellious Heart

The Michigan Brides Collection
Unending Devotion
A Noble Groom
Captured by Love

Historical
Luther and Katharina
Newton & Polly

ENRICHED

KNIGHTS OF 4 BRETHREN

JODY HEDLUND

NORTHERN LIGHTS PRESS

Enriched
Northern Lights Press
© 2022 Copyright
Jody Hedlund
Jody Hedlund Print Edition

ISBN 979-8-9852649-1-3

www.jodyhedlund.com

Scripture quotations are taken from the King James Version of the Bible.

This is a work of historical reconstruction; the appearances of certain historical figures are accordingly inevitable. All other characters are products of the author's imagination. Any resemblance to actual events or locales or persons, living or dead, is entirely coincidental.

Cover Design by Roseanna White Designs
Cover images from Shutterstock
Interior Map Design by Jenna Hedlund

TUNDRA SEA
N
W   E
S
St. Olaf's
Abbey
Frozen
Wilds
The Hundreds
Finnmark
SNOWDEN
MOUNTAIN
RANGE
SWAINE
Golden
Plateau
NORVEGIA
DARK SEA
HARDANGER FOREST
Romsdal
ATLAS RIVER
Moors of
Many Lakes
BLOOD RIVER
Wahlburg
Castle
Valley of
Red Dragons
Richlande
Lowlands
Vordinberg
Bay of
Fire
Ostby
Sound
Cimbrian
Strait
WHITE SEA
UTHELANDE
Cimbrian Peninsula
THE WEND

Chapter 1

TORVALD

I LOATHED THE SIGHT OF WAHLBURG CASTLE.

I halted my mount in the river bottom, rested my reins on my thigh, and turned a critical eye upon my boyhood home and the estate I would one day inherit.

Perched upon a steep rocky cliff that bordered the Blood River, the fortress was impenetrable on the two sides built against the cliffs. If an enemy attacked, they would have to attempt a takeover by way of the southern and eastern portions, which were fortified with thick double walls that rose higher than any ladder or siege engine could span.

If only my father hadn't allowed the place to fall into such disrepair . . .

The crenellations were crumbling. The arrow slits were collapsing. One of the turrets was tottering. The family banner streaming from a spiral tower roof was in tatters. The emblem of a bear standing with claws extended—representing strength, cunning, and ferocity— was barely recognizable. The once-bright green background—that stood for hope, joy, and loyalty in love—was now faded to a pale olive.

I expelled a bitter breath. Nothing regarding my family crest was true, especially of my father. He had no strength, cunning, or ferocity. And he certainly had no hope or joy. The only trait he maintained was loyalty in love, much to his detriment. He'd remained loyal in love to my mother, even though she'd abandoned him many years ago when she'd run away with another nobleman.

His undying obsession over her had been his downfall, had led to a melancholy so great that he'd ceased living and had instead wallowed in despair. Thereafter, he was as broken and in as much disrepair as the fortress.

At a splatter of a raindrop against my face, I nudged my horse toward the pathway that led up to the gatehouse. Behind me, the clomping of hooves indicated that my squires were following closely.

Our surcoats contained the king's emblem—dragon heads on a background of royal red—designating us as the king's men. As my most trusted squires, they'd been with me throughout the winter and spring during the search for the sacred chalice on behalf of King Ansgar, who was desperate to find the ancient relic with the hope it could bring healing to his wife, Queen Lis, who was perishing from a bleeding disease.

I was grateful for the quiet, steady presence of my squires during this difficult homecoming. Even so, I regretted not accepting Gunnar's offer to come with me. Instead, I'd encouraged my fellow Knight of Brethren to remain in Romsdal and continue looking for the chalice without me. I'd assured him I would return in a fortnight.

Two weeks was sufficient for the task at hand. In fact, it was overlong.

Any amount of time was too lengthy for a wedding I didn't want to a woman I didn't know.

I was tempted to do my duty tonight and leave on the morrow. But I had too much principle and would force myself to remain for a polite duration.

Another raindrop hit my face. At the darkening clouds overhead, I nudged my mount to a faster pace. The April afternoon was almost spent, and I wasn't surprised a spring storm was greeting my arrival home. It was all too fitting.

Dusty and gritty from the past couple of days of hard riding, I drew up the hood of my cloak over my chain mail. With each plodding step up the path, my heart sank lower. By the time we reached the gatehouse, the heaviness inside threatened to hold me back.

Though the portcullis was raised, I reined in. Upon the high plateau of the riverbank, the wind slapped against me, the coldness reminding me of the long winter we'd endured. Now, with the coming of spring, 'twould not be long ere King Canute rallied his army and attacked Norvegia again. The Swainian king had a grandmother who'd been a royal Norwegian princess. Because of his connection to the Oldenberg bloodline, he insisted he was the rightful heir to Norvegia's throne.

Our scouts were keeping an eye on King Canute's movements. And once he launched his initiative, I intended to join in, even though custom dictated that an elite Knight of Brethren who took a wife was to resign from the king's service. I prayed no one would object to my continuing as a Brethren, at least until King Canute was defeated.

While I'd hoped to serve King Ansgar for many more years, I'd been born and bred to be an obedient son. I understood that as the future heir of Wahlburg, I had an obligation to take a wife and have a family. Now that my father had summoned me home to wed, I would do as he had requested, even though it was the last thing I wanted to do.

Peering through the gatehouse past the outer bailey and into the inner courtyard, I could see a group of people congregated outside the central doors of the main building of the keep. Clearly, the guards on lookout had seen us coming for some time and had made the announcement of our approach.

I couldn't hold back a scowl. I didn't want to be greeted by anyone, not household staff and certainly not by strangers—including my future wife and her kin. No doubt this was Ingold's doing. The steward had likely brought our dwindling fortune to my father's attention, suggested I marry someone with a large dowry who could restore our wealth, and then sought the best candidate. In addition, Ingold had probably made all the preparations for the maiden's visit.

All my father did—in addition to wasting our fortune— was nod his permission. Yes, he excelled at wasting things—time, wealth, land, lives... and love over a woman who hadn't deserved it.

I ducked my head to hide my irritation and steered my horse into the fortress, praying for the strength to be patient over the coming days. I knew people talked about my ruthlessness in battle as well as my brooding and severe nature. The rumors weren't false. I was a hard man.

But for today, for a fortnight, I had to temper myself and remain gracious as best I was able. I'd had to do so on other occasions, like the week I participated in Princess

Elinor's courtship last autumn. As one of twelve noblemen chosen to compete for her affection and the position of future king, I'd gone to Vordinberg and done what was expected of me, although I'd had no heart for the challenges or for her.

As I drew nigh the keep, the wind picked up and brought with it more rain.

"Greetings, my lord." Ingold stood at the forefront of the gathering, the wind threatening to blow away his diminutive, lean frame. He clung to his hood, anchoring it in place over his bald head. "Welcome home."

I nodded at the middle-aged steward my father had appointed to run Wahlburg estate many years ago. As a former Sagacite, he was an intelligent man. If only he had the courage to put an end to my father's foolish use of Wahlburg's resources.

Alas, now the burden was upon my shoulders to save my father and our family name from utter ruin by marrying a wealthy noblewoman. What did I have to offer the maiden and her kin in return? What had Ingold bargained?

The question had nagged me throughout the ride back. I not only planned to find out, but I also needed to take time during my stay to investigate the ledgers and put an end to the wastefulness so that we didn't find ourselves in this same financial ruin again one day.

I slid from my horse. Before I had the chance to straighten and take a breath, Ingold was waving his hand at the group behind him, nearly a dozen noblemen and women along with their servants. "I am very pleased to introduce you to Lord Royse, my lord."

A large man with a hefty girth stepped forward. He wore a flat hat over bright red curly hair. His big face was made even bigger by a bushy beard as fiery as his hair. He carried himself with an imposing air, but it was his clothing that made him stand apart. His cloak was thick and finely embroidered. The surcoat underneath was of the richest quality linen, woven with a myriad of colors, including golden thread. His leather belt, calf-length boots, and gloves all appeared new and of excellent quality.

"Lord Torvald." The man spoke reverently and with a bow, almost as if I were royalty. "It is a great honor to meet you. Great honor, indeed. We are familiar with all the tales of your renown and heroic deeds."

I bowed my head in return. I never knew how to respond to the flattery bestowed upon me since becoming a Knight of Brethren. Being singled out made me uncomfortable, so most of the time, I ignored the comments.

"We thank you for inviting us here to Wahlburg and considering the possibility of a union." He slid a glance to the women clustered behind him. "I hope you will find Lady Karina to your liking and will agree to take her as your wife."

So, the deal wasn't solidified? I caught Ingold's gaze. I'd assumed I was all but married to the maiden he'd selected for me. Was I to have some say in the matter after all?

Ingold wasn't paying me heed, was instead beaming at Lord Royse, as if he was the savior come to deliver us from all our woes.

What did it matter if I liked Lord Royse's daughter? Hadn't I told myself many times that whether I liked my wife or not was of no consequence? In fact, I would prefer not to find her attractive and appealing. Then I would have no reason to fear having my heart broken and turning into my father.

It was for the best to have a loveless arranged marriage, to remain unattached and aloof. Besides, I needed to stay focused on the other tasks that required my attention during my brief time home.

Even so, I couldn't keep my gaze from shifting to the women Lord Royse had referenced. Two were standing directly behind him. A petite woman wore a nun's habit, and a wimple surrounded her head, covering her hair. As the wind blew at her, she wrestled with the veil that was blowing over her eyes and across her face, obscuring her from view.

Why had a nun accompanied Lord Royse? Was she a personal attendant to Lady Karina?

With a knot forming in my stomach, one that I could only attribute to nervousness, I forced my gaze to the second woman, Lady Karina. At the sight of her face, the coils inside me unraveled. Her unremarkable brown hair was styled simply. Her brown-green eyes, while kind, did not draw me in. And though another man might consider her features pretty, I found nothing in her face that would make me want to take a second look. She, like her father, was stockier of frame and attired in fine garments, although hers were much simpler and less elegant.

I didn't let my gaze linger over her. I'd seen enough to know I needn't worry about falling for her. She was a perfect candidate for becoming my wife.

Wife. The word pricked me. Even if she wasn't someone I had to worry about losing my heart to, did I really need to get married now? Could I wait a few more years? Was the financial situation so dire that I must marry immediately?

From the outside, the castle was in disrepair. What about the inside?

Lord Royse was talking about their travels south from Finnmark. I listened with one ear while, with a sinking heart, I took in the demise all around. The thatched roofs of the outbuildings needed repairs. The inner bailey wall was crumbling, similar to the battlements. Shutters on the keep were hanging at angles or gone altogether. Even the once-thriving garden and orchard were overgrown and in need of pruning.

I'd noticed the deterioration last autumn when I'd returned home for a short visit after being sent away from court. I'd known the coffers were dwindling. But the truth was that the estate had been declining for years. I'd simply been too preoccupied by other duties to pay heed.

Now, faced with the imminent prospect of having to get married to save my family home, I could no longer overlook the problems and only wished I'd done more sooner to stave off the predicament in which I found myself.

A crack of thunder split the air, and the rain began in earnest. Lord Royse and the others took that as their cue to race up the stone stairs and into the castle. I didn't watch their retreat. Instead, I led my mount toward the stables and extinguished the last flicker of hope I'd allowed myself to harbor—the hope that the need to get married had been a mistake.

However, my father had truly and utterly brought not only himself to ruin, but he'd done so with Wahlburg. Now I was left with no choice but to salvage the wreckage. I would have to get married. There was no way around it.

Chapter
2

"Your father will want to see you right away, my lord." Ingold scrambled to keep up with my long stride down the passageway toward my chamber. "And then you will want to bathe before the feast tonight."

"I would prefer a quiet supper." The wall sconces were lit but did little to chase away the shadows the storm had brought.

"We must entertain our guests properly. A wealthy family like the Royses are accustomed to a more lavish lifestyle."

"Very well." I pushed down the frustration that had been building since the moment I'd stepped into the keep and Ingold began bombarding me with a list of expectations.

"I made arrangements for a harpist to provide music."

"And the wedding?" I held back a shudder at the mere mention of the word. "Is that tonight as well?"

"No, we shall wait until the morrow. That will give us more time to prepare all the courses necessary for the wedding supper as well as a dance afterward."

The tension inside loosened a little. "Can we afford the *lavishness?*"

"If you seal this union, then yes."

I halted abruptly and spun on Ingold. "I assumed the union was sealed already."

At least a foot shorter than my towering build, my father's steward peered up at me, rubbing a hand over his bald head as was his habit when he was nervous. "I have done my best to win Lord Royse and Lady Karina over, my lord. Now the rest is in your hands."

"So, there is still a chance they may decide against the marriage?"

"'Tis unlikely. But yes. Lord Royse is used to giving in to the whims of his daughter. As much as Lord Royse wants this arrangement, he won't force his daughter into it."

I knew almost nothing about Lord Royse. But his sensitivity to his daughter in the choice of a marriage partner was a quality I could respect. Women needed to have a voice in whom they married. Perhaps if my mother had been allowed more freedom, she would have had fewer regrets.

Whatever the case, I wanted to know more about the Royses. "What exactly do they stand to gain from marriage to me?"

Ingold swept his gaze over the passageway as though checking to be sure we were alone. Then he leaned closer. "Lord Royse aspires for a position on the Noble Council."

The annoyance roiling around inside swirled faster. "You know I have no control over who may or may not be on the Noble Council." I was close to the king, but he was first and foremost my trusted friend. And I wouldn't use the association to my advantage.

"I realize that, my lord. And I informed Lord Royse of the same. Even if he cannot be on the Noble Council, he would be happy with the prestige and power he will gain by his association with you."

"So he wants more prestige and power?"

"After years of success with his textiles, Lord Royse has more riches than he knows what to do with. However, he's failed to gain the notoriety and respect due a man of his wealth. His daughter's union to you would change that entirely."

Indeed, his connection to me would give him the recognition he sought. Everyone would learn of his name and 'twould likely benefit his textile efforts all the more. "And what of the lady? What does she hope to gain?"

Ingold hesitated in his response, enough for me to know Lady Karina was less willing than her father. "I believe she would like to make her father happy."

"And that is all?"

The patter of rain against a nearby leaded windowpane filled the silence. "She'll see soon enough that you are a handsome man, and she will be smitten with you, just like all the other maidens in Norvegia."

I couldn't hold back a snort at Ingold's exaggeration. I started forward again.

"My lord, you must do your best to be charming tonight," he called after me.

I was not now and never would be charming. "If she does not like me for who I am, then I will not wed her."

Ingold's footsteps slapped rapidly in his attempt to catch up. "We do not have the time or means to invite additional marriageable candidates to Wahlburg."

At the gravity in Ingold's voice, I slowed my pace. His

warning came through clearly: Lady Karina might be my only chance at saving Wahlburg. If I didn't impress her this eve, she wouldn't want to marry me. And if she didn't marry me, she'd leave and take the Royse fortune with her.

"I know you dislike social gatherings." Ingold softened his tone. "But you must do your best to win her over."

So, I had to pretend to be interested in Lady Karina? Pretend I was attracted? Pretend I anticipated a future with her? When the truth was that I would be glad of the day in a fortnight when I could ride away and leave her behind.

I didn't want to be duplicitous with any woman and lead her to believe I'd care about her when I never would. But what choice did I have?

Ahead, an arched stone doorway signified the chapel. The door was slightly ajar. It seemed to beckon to me almost urgently to spend a few minutes in prayer before visiting my father and before beginning the charade with the woman I needed to marry.

I stalked toward it, anxious to be away from Ingold and his plans and schedules and admonishments. As I stopped abruptly in front of the door, he bumped into me.

"My lord—"

I cast him a dark gaze, and he shrank back. Knowing I'd gained for myself only a temporary reprieve, I entered and closed the door.

Quieting my steps and my heart, I let the coldness of the room soothe me. Not until I was halfway down the aisle did I realize that someone else was already making use of the sanctuary and kneeling at the prayer rail. The light from a lone altar candle fell across the occupant, revealing the long, flowing habit and veil belonging to a nun—the nun who had accompanied Lady Karina.

I almost halted, most surely stumbled. For an instant I considered turning around and leaving. I had no wish to interrupt this holy woman's time of prayer. But in the next moment, I pushed forward. This was my home and my chapel. I had every right to the solitude of the sacred place. If she didn't like my presence, then she could leave.

She twisted her head around to view me, then sucked in a sharp breath.

I kept my attention focused on the cross hanging above the altar. Maybe if I didn't spare her a glance, she would quietly finish her prayers and be on her way without disturbing me.

But with every step I took, I could feel her examining me with open curiosity.

When I reached the rail, I made sure I was as far from her as possible. Then I lowered myself to my knees on the prayer cushion, folded my hands over the rail, and bowed my head. From the corner of my eye, I could see that she had turned squarely to face me. In fact, she was making no secret of scrutinizing me from my head to my boots.

I closed my eyes. Surely she would respect the peace of the chapel and wouldn't attempt to make conversation. Weren't nuns supposed to be silent anyway?

I had no reason to be concerned. She would get up in a moment and leave me undisturbed. But even as I attempted to calm my spirit and focus on my prayer, I could feel her attention riveted to me as if I were a saint in the flesh.

Should I cast her a glare like the one I'd just given to Ingold? That would send her scurrying from my presence.

I shot a dark look her way, catching sight of a pretty

face—one with elegantly defined features, long lashes, and a sprinkling of freckles across her nose and cheeks.

After everything Ingold had said of the need to woo Lady Karina, I could ill afford to send this nun running off and telling tales of my rudeness. Perhaps I needed to make use of the occasion to find out more about the lady so that I might be better prepared this eve when I spoke with her at the feast.

The problem was, I'd never been proficient at interacting with women. In fact, other than my week with Princess Elinor last autumn, I'd avoided all engagements with the ladies at court. Ansgar and I had been of the same mind, retiring to our quarters together while the other knights fraternized with lovely maidens who were eager to spend time with knights like us.

What should I say to this servant? My mind scrambled for some topic of conversation. But I could think of nothing. Not one single thing.

If I was having this much trouble with Lady Karina's nun, what would I be like with the lady herself? 'Twould be a long night ahead.

Frustration buzzed around my chest, like hornets disturbed from their nest. I hated that my father had placed me in this situation. If only he'd been a stronger man, I wouldn't be here.

I might be stuck repairing all his mistakes. But I would never make them for myself. Especially falling in love with a woman.

Chapter 3

Karina

Torvald Wahlburg was more handsome in person than I'd expected. In spite of all I'd heard about him, I still wasn't prepared for his good looks. And now seeing him this close from my prayer cushion, my thoughts scattered like seed pearls spilling over the floor.

Earlier outside, I hadn't been able to view him well, not only because his hood had concealed him but because the wind had decided to torment me by blowing my garments into a storm of their own.

Now that he was without his cloak, I could see that his hair was dark brown, neatly trimmed, and slightly damp. His jaw was square, his cheeks chiseled, his forehead and nose perfectly proportioned. The slight scar on his cheek added to his appeal—although I didn't quite know why.

I tugged at my habit tangling in my legs and tried to position myself more comfortably. I should have changed from the nun's clothing as Marta had suggested. My maidservant had warned me I would be more comfortable in something else, but I hadn't been ready to relinquish the garments that had been a part of my life for the past three years.

In fact, as much as I wanted to make my father happy, I'd been hesitant ever since he'd ridden up to the convent and asked me to give up my aspirations of becoming a nun and to marry Lord Torvald instead. After having resigned myself to a life behind the convent walls, I'd expected to live out the rest of my days as a single woman. I'd never imagined getting married, much less to a man like Torvald.

Even in our remote northern convent, we'd heard about the noblemen who'd taken part in Princess Elinor's courtship week. As noblewomen, we'd been familiar with the men who'd been chosen to participate.

Of course, our conversations had been whispered in secret where our superiors wouldn't be able to hear us going on about the knights. And although all of us had known we'd never be able to entertain thoughts of a man for ourselves, that hadn't stopped us from fantasizing over the knights for the princess.

We were happy Princess Elinor had found the true love of her life with Maxim and that the two now served together, advising the king and queen. Even if Torvald hadn't ended up with the princess, we'd still gossiped about him from time to time. He remained popular among most maidens, which was why my father's request that I marry Torvald had come as such a shock . . . and still was.

Why would such a coveted man marry a woman like me? Yes, I knew it was because his family needed the wealth of my dowry. Father had already spoken of the agreement. But Torvald could have won the hand of a more coveted wealthy woman. He didn't have to settle for me.

"Indeed. You are every bit as handsome as everyone has said." The words slipped out before I could censure myself. Inwardly, I sighed. What was wrong with me that I could never speak without making a fool of myself? Now that I'd uttered something so forward, I needed to explain myself. "Not that I've been speaking with everyone. Not at all. I overheard the other postulants expounding upon your attributes. I thought they were exaggerating, but I can see now that they were not."

With his head bent and eyes closed, Torvald didn't move, except that his jaw flexed.

I was rambling. Wasn't I? It was another one of my faults.

"Forgive me for focusing on your outward appearance. I imagine you are just as brave, kind, and noble as you are handsome. And those qualities are of equal importance."

He cracked open an eye and slid a sideways glance at me.

If only Marta were with me. Even though she was a servant, she was my closest companion and had accompanied me to the convent and attended to me there. Older than my eighteen by several years, she was more knowledgeable in the ways of men, since she hadn't needed to live under the strict convent regulations regarding chastity and segregation.

Ever since I'd agreed to my father's plan to wed Torvald, I'd been plying her with questions about how to interact with men, and she'd readily shared her wisdom.

What would she have me say now to Torvald instead of rambling on like a lunatic? I glanced to the closed chapel door and willed her to walk through at that moment.

Alas, the door didn't budge.

I wrapped my leather belt around my finger, then unwound it. "So, are you excited about the wedding on the morrow?"

Although his eyes were no longer closed, his head remained bent.

Had I uttered another inane question? Maybe he wasn't excited about the wedding. After all, I knew a great deal of information about him, but he likely knew very little about me. "Forgive me. How can you be excited about marrying a woman you do not know?"

"Tell me about Lady Karina." His command was gruff. "Please," he added as though recognizing his tone.

Why was he referring to me as though I weren't present in the chapel? Perhaps this was an easier way for him to converse. "Well . . . what would you like to know about *Lady Karina*?"

"Anything." He stared down at his folded hands. His fingers were long. With so fierce a reputation, what would his touch be like?

My insides quavered. Although I was naïve about men in many ways, I understood that once I was married, I would have new expectations placed upon me, namely sharing my husband's bed and bearing him children, especially a son to carry on his title. The very prospect sent embarrassment rushing through me as it had the few other occasions my mind had wandered that direction. 'Twas no easy task switching from thinking I'd remain chaste for my whole life to realizing I'd now have marital duties.

He shot me a glance.

Could he sense the direction my thoughts had just veered?

Mortification pumped heat into my cheeks. I had to say something, change the subject. "Very well. I—Lady Karina loves the color gold. She adores goldenrod and loosestrife. Golden apples are her favorite fruit. And she likes the sky at sunrise because of the golden hues."

His lips pressed into a thin line.

Had I overshared? My tendency to do so was as strong as my tendency to ramble.

"Is she excited about the wedding?" he asked softly.

"She is nervous." Yes, this conversation in the third person was easier. "She does not know if she is doing the right thing."

He was silent.

Maybe he didn't like my answer. Maybe I should have been more positive. Even if I was nervous and not sure whether I was doing the right thing, my time at the convent over recent months had grown increasingly difficult. The painful bruises on my back were all the reminder I needed that cloistered life hadn't gone the way I'd hoped. "Even if she is nervous and unsure, she is hoping the change is a good one."

"What can I do to help make it good?" With this question, he shifted and glanced at me more fully.

I found myself looking into his serious, solemn, and soulful eyes. Although the darkness obscured the color, nothing could diminish the magnetism. It wrapped around me, held me fast, and cut off my breath.

Saints and angels. No wonder so many women fawned over him. His gorgeous eyes alone had the power to take a maiden captive.

Before I'd entered the convent at fifteen, I'd had only a few men pay attention to me. Of course, I'd been young, and Father hadn't been in a hurry to wed me off and so hadn't given me many opportunities to meet men. On the rare occasions I'd mingled at parties or dances, I'd drawn stares. All because of my long curly red hair. It was wild and untamable, reaching past my waist.

Marta had insisted I leave my hair long until I took my vows, when I'd be required to shear off the locks and wear my hair short, as was the custom of the nuns. Marta had helped me conceal my red hair under my wimple so that at times I almost forgot about it.

If I was completely honest, I suspected part of the reason I hadn't wanted to shed my wimple for the greeting with Torvald outside was because I didn't want to frighten him away with my red hair. If I could have a chance to impress him first, then maybe he'd be more accepting of my hair.

He cocked an eyebrow.

"Oh yes." He'd asked me a question. But what? "You're wanting to know how to make this change good?"

He waited without answering.

"Hmmm . . ." I looped my belt around my finger again. "Be genuinely yourself. Whenever someone is new, it always helps when other people are genuine."

He pushed himself quickly to his feet, something akin to chagrin flashing across his face. Without another glance, he spun and stalked down the aisle.

"Wait." What had I said wrong? Had I offended him? "I can tell you more."

"No." The word was hard, almost angry. "'Tis not necessary."

I scrambled up, grabbing onto the prayer rail to keep from tripping in the folds of my habit. I'd never mastered the womanly art of gracefulness, not even at the convent where we'd been required to move slowly and carefully.

"What will make the change good for you?" I tossed out the only question I could think of.

He reached the door and paused. "Tell your mistress I will do my best to be genuine."

Mistress? My lips stalled around my request for him to stay longer. Why did he think I had a mistress?

He fled from the chapel before I could find my voice. I didn't lose it too oft. In fact, I was rarely without something to say. But in this case, I could only stare at the closed door. Had Torvald not realized my identity as Lady Karina?

I plumped out the habit that fell to my feet and concealed every inch of my body. 'Twas possible in my nun's attire he'd mistaken me as a maidservant or companion for Lady Karina.

"Of course. Leave it to me to get myself into this embarrassing predicament." My future husband—the incredibly good-looking man I was marrying on the morrow—had no idea I was his bride.

"After admonishing him to be genuine, now I shall arrive at the festivities tonight, and he will assume I was ingenuine with him, pretending to be someone I was not." With a groan, I buried my face into my hands. If he'd been hesitant to marry me before, this would only make things worse.

Should I continue wearing my nun's clothing? Perpetuate the charade, perhaps just for this evening?

"No!" The vehemence of the word echoed against the stone walls. Why was I even considering such a scheme? It was one thing to have a case of mistaken identity. But it was another altogether to willfully lie about myself. Dishonesty was a grievous way to start a relationship. Besides, my father, my brother, sister-in-law, and several other members of our household had accompanied me to Wahlburg. They would surely give away my identity within minutes.

"Devils and demons, Karina." I dropped my voice. Even so, it was fraught with censure. "Can you not go one day without botching something?"

I stared down at my habit. As the youngest child, I'd always struggled with feeling ignored by my family. Of course, I didn't blame them at all. They'd poured out their attention upon my mother—and rightly so—after she started having seizures. Although I'd tried to be as quiet and reserved as my mother needed, I'd failed in that regard.

When I entered the convent, I'd hoped my going away would afford her more peace. And when I donned the habit, I'd also hoped I could finally conceal my flaws. I wasn't sure I'd accomplished either objective. My mother had died only months after I left, and my flaws had trailed me, causing me trouble.

As scared as I was to put aside the clothing, it was time to stop hiding behind the head-to-toe covering. I needed to enlist Marta's aid in making myself as presentable as possible. If she styled my hair with jewels or flowers or both, we could camouflage most of the red. Perhaps then I wouldn't scare Torvald away . . . if I hadn't already done so.

Chapter 4

TORVALD

I PRESSED A KISS AGAINST MY FATHER'S CLAMMY HAND, THEN gently lowered it back to the bed at his side.

He was much worse than I'd expected.

"Please, my lord." Ingold stood near the door, and his whisper needled me. "The guests are waiting; the first course is ready. You must go now."

After bathing and grooming, I'd had little time left for this visit to my father's chamber. But I'd stopped, heedless of Ingold's prompting me to do so later.

I straightened, watching the emaciated face of my father for a flicker of awakening. With sunken cheeks and hollowed eyes, his face was as boney and thin as the rest of his body—the outline visible beneath the sheet that covered him. His skin was mottled gray and his hair and beard white, making him appear much older than his fifty years.

The strong scent of incense in the air was meant to ward off the melancholy that had plagued my father these many years. But the spicy aroma hadn't helped. Nor had the copious amounts of wine he drank.

I'd tried everything as a lad to give him motivation to carry on with his life. A primary reason I'd worked so hard to become one of the best knights in Norvegia was to make him proud. I'd even agreed to the courtship week for Princess Elinor, thinking that if I won and became the next king, my father would finally rouse from his stupor and find purpose again.

But nothing had ever brought my father out of his despondency.

The large canopy over the bed and the half-closed bed curtains cast a shadow over him. Truthfully, he was nothing but a shadow himself. Even if he awoke, he wouldn't be able to join in the feast tonight. And from all appearances, he wouldn't be able to attend the wedding on the morrow either.

I bowed my head, not wanting to feel anything but anger. But sorrow invaded my soul. I was sad for the wasted years, the wasted life. I wished there was something more I could do to help him. But I was beginning to accept that I could not help a man who didn't want to help himself.

Ingold cleared his throat.

I took a last look at my father only to see a silver chain slipping out from underneath his tunic. Upon the chain, he wore the wedding band he'd once given to my mother. The one she'd left behind.

I fisted my fingers to keep from reaching down, jerking the necklace free, and throwing it into the closest privy. He'd held on to the ring and her for too long. Why couldn't he let her go?

With a frustrated growl, I spun on my heels, stalked to the door, and flung it open. My father was a simpering, weak fool. And I vowed as I had already dozens of times that I would never turn into him, especially never allowing myself to love a woman and chance being hurt the way he had.

"The flowers, my lord." Ingold raced to stay beside me and thrust a bouquet into my hands.

At the sight of the requested golden flowers, I recoiled and pushed them back at him. "You deliver them to her."

Ingold fumbled and nearly dropped them. "'Twould mean more to the lady if you gave them yourself."

Heat stole up my neck, and I was glad for the dimness of the passageway that hid my embarrassment. I didn't want to arrive in the great hall carrying flowers. But at the same time, I was plagued with the admonition from the conversation I'd had earlier with Lady Karina's servant in the chapel. *"Be genuinely yourself. Whenever someone is new, it always helps when other people are genuine."*

After visiting my father and renewing my vow never to care about a woman, what could be less genuine than giving the lady flowers and engaging in small talk with the hope of making her like me when all along I had no plans to like her in return?

I expelled a frustrated breath.

Ingold pushed the flowers toward me again. "I have no doubt you'll be able to convince her to go through with the arrangement, my lord."

He was right. It was an arrangement, nothing more than a business transaction. I'd assure her that I'd be a kind man, never misuse her, and treat her with respect. I'd also do everything in my power to make sure she was happy and well taken care of. Surely she would be satisfied with that. It was more than many women could hope for from their husbands in an arranged marriage.

As we arrived at the open double doors of the great hall, I straightened my tunic made of fine royal blue that fell to my knees but slit a few inches up the sides revealing my woolen leggings. Over the top of the tunic, I wore a mid-thigh cote that buttoned up the front and showed off my muscular form. My leather belt hung at my hips and contained my sword—something I was never without. I'd preferred to wear my comfortable boots, but Ingold had presented me with a new pair with thick, sturdy laces.

Therewith, I felt like a shiny relic on display, something that everyone might examine and admire. And I wished I hadn't taken so much care with my appearance.

"You'll do fine, my lord." Ingold patted my back as though I were a child instead of a full-grown man.

Shaking off his hand, I pushed forward into the hall. As the glow of the candelabras on each table illuminated my presence, the chatter faded into silence.

I didn't glance around, didn't want to see who was in attendance. Instead, I strode past the side trestle tables and made my way to the dais. I focused on the empty spot at the center of the head table, one normally reserved for my father but that now belonged to me.

Upon reaching the open floor in front of the dais, I searched the guests at the head table. They'd arisen out of respect, and I had no trouble locating Lord Royse with his red hair and beard and wearing another extravagant outfit that was elaborately embroidered.

"Lord Royse." I nodded my acknowledgment. "I welcome you again to Wahlburg."

"Thank you, Lord Torvald." He nodded in return, his eyes alight with an eagerness I couldn't miss. It was obvious he wanted this union and the prestige it would bring him.

"Lady Karina." I shifted so that I was facing the chair on the opposite side of the center, the one where I knew Ingold had placed Lady Karina. The young woman standing there curtsied and bowed her head.

For a moment, I could only stare at her hair. Even though it was pulled up into plaited coils and was covered with a caul of lace and pearls, there was no hiding the bright red color. It flamed as if it were on fire.

Where was the brown?

I let my gaze drift over the rest of her. Gone was the stocky frame, and in its place was a lithe but curvaceous body in a form-fitting gown of purple, embroidered with intricate patterns of gold. Though petite, she radiated an energy and vivaciousness that sent alarm clanging through me.

What had happened to the plain, unassuming woman from earlier?

As Lady Karina straightened and lifted her head, I nearly faltered at the sight of her face, one dusted with enchanting freckles. The bright blue eyes peering at me belonged to the nun who'd been praying in the chapel. The servant. The companion to Lady Karina.

Why was she now posing as the lady herself?

The luminous eyes filled with an apology. An apology for what?

In an instant I knew. This was no servant. This was Lady Karina and had been all along. Somehow during our exchange, she'd discovered I'd mistaken her for her servant. But she hadn't corrected me, had instead allowed me to make a fool of myself. And now she was apologizing.

I quickly reined in my emotions, keeping my expression as stoic as always. This was exactly the duplicitous nature I deplored, the kind that reminded me of my mother. Apparently, Providence was refusing to grant my wish to marry a plain woman. But at least if I must wed an exceptionally comely one, I would have no trouble disliking her. In fact, perhaps eventually I would loathe her as much as I loathed my mother.

I was tempted to toss the bouquet on the table in front of Lady Karina. But I held it out politely. "For you, lady." I still had a job to do tonight. I would play this little game with her and somehow win.

Her lips curved into a hesitant smile, and even though small, the smile added to her beguile. "They are beautiful, my lord. And golden." Her voice contained a breathiness that would have turned any other man to clay. But not me. I stiffened my spine. I would never let a woman like this mold me.

"I was informed Lady Karina liked the color gold." I couldn't keep the edge from my tone.

Her lashes fell, and her cheeks flushed a becoming hue. When she glanced up a second later, her eyes pleaded with me again to forgive her. The blue was like that of a sky after a rainstorm—clear, cloudless, wide open.

She buried her nose in the bouquet. When she looked up again, her smile widened into one that was utterly irresistible, one that made me want to give her flowers every day just so I could behold her smile. But of course, I wouldn't.

"Thank you, Lord Torvald. I could ask for no greater kindness and thoughtfulness."

I bowed my head curtly, then headed toward the steps and ascended the dais. I could feel her gaze following me, but even when I brushed past her and took my chair, I refused to look at her. The less I gave in to the desire to study her, the better I'd be able to resist a physical attraction.

As I took my seat, everyone else sat back down. Lady Karina resumed her place beside me, still holding the flowers. Her slender fingers wrapped around the stems tightly, turning her knuckles white. Was she nervous too?

I needed to make conversation with her and put her at ease. But I couldn't make myself speak with her. Instead, I posed a question to her father.

Lord Royse needed very little prompting to start talking. During the first and second courses, he spoke enthusiastically of his textile industry, the growing of flax, the special dye he made from the golden lichen that grew on the rocks and trees on his land, the vast production of cloth he'd developed that used the golden threads, and the growing demand and popularity of his cloth.

By the time the servants brought out the third course—the roasted sparrows, baked quinces, and fruit compotes—guilt hammered at my conscience. I was being a donkey toward Lady Karina. If she was to be my wife—and according to Ingold she was my best option—then I needed to figure out a way to relate to her, since I couldn't spend the rest of my life avoiding her.

As Ingold stepped up to Lord Royse to speak with him, he slanted me a chastising look, one that told me he'd noticed I was ignoring Lady Karina and that he'd interfered so that I would pay the lady some attention. If I didn't, I would risk losing her altogether. And I couldn't afford that. The future of Wahlburg depended upon her.

I adjusted in my chair to converse with her. Her trencher was still filled from the second course, which meant she'd eaten hardly anything. Her slender fingers fiddled with her fork. The flowers lay on the table in front of her, now slightly wilted.

She was making small talk with the lady beside her, who was a cousin or sister or sister-in-law or some relation to the Royse family.

As I cleared my throat, Lady Karina stopped her exchange mid-sentence and cast a glance at me.

"Lady Karina, do you make a habit of visiting chapels disguised as a nun?" The moment the question was out, I wished I could take it back, especially with so hard an edge. I could have asked her about her journey here, or about the weather, or even how she was enjoying the meal. Instead, I went directly for the issue at hand, never one to circumvent a problem.

"Yes." Her tone was sincere with almost a pleading quality to it. "For the past three years, I have dressed as a nun—a postulant, actually."

Surprise jolted through me as quick as a lightning strike. As much as I wanted to avert eye contact, I found myself staring at her lovely face, her eyes wide with remorse.

"I sincerely wish I had shed my postulant attire the day I left the convent as my father requested, but giving up my aspiration to become a nun is proving more difficult than I imagined it would be."

Lady Karina had lived in a convent and had been planning to become a nun? When had she left? And why? As much as I wanted to blurt the questions, my tongue was suddenly bridled.

She rubbed her sleeves, as though feeling bare without her habit. "I regret the confusion I caused you, my lord. I truly did not realize you mistook me for a servant until you were leaving the chapel and instructed me to tell my mistress you would be genuine. Only then did I comprehend that you did not know my identity."

A part of me was relieved Lady Karina seemed to be as talkative as her father and that I need not loosen my tongue to respond.

"The moment I realized the mistake, I should have raced after you. I beg you to forgive me for not doing so. I regret that I was the one who was not genuine after my suggestion to you."

This wasn't all her fault. I'd been quick to judge her without knowing all the facts.

She dropped her attention to her fork, and she began flipping the utensil over and back again.

"Do you still wish to be a nun?" After she'd apologized so sincerely, I needed to do likewise, but I couldn't contain my blunt nature.

She paused in twisting her fork and lifted a hand to her chest, spreading it above her bodice, trying but unable to cover the leagues of creamy skin brushed with more enchanting freckles.

As if noticing my scrutiny, she removed her hand. "I am not accustomed to showing so much of myself. After the past years in my wimple and habit, I feel rather bare tonight."

Bare? The mere mention of such a word conjured forbidden images. I quickly stabbed the tip of my knife into something on my plate and brought it to my mouth, not knowing or caring what it was.

"Saints and angels." She pressed her hand to her chest again. "Forgive me for speaking so brazenly. I am sorely out of practice at being in mixed company."

I ripped off a chunk of meat, tasting nothing and trying desperately not to let my gaze or thoughts wander back to her chest.

"I admit," she continued, "I was surprised when my father arrived at the convent and asked me to do this for him."

Ingold had indicated that Lord Royse wouldn't force his daughter into a marriage, that she'd gone along with his plans to make him happy. But if she truly wanted to be a nun, then I wouldn't agree to this marriage even if she was the last eligible woman in Norvegia. I couldn't tear a woman away from serving in the church if that was her deepest desire.

"You have yet to answer my question, lady." I jabbed my knife into another piece of meat. "Do you or do you not want to become a nun?"

"'Tis complicated, my lord—"

"I shall not stand in the way of a calling to serve God."

"Thank you. I own freely that I am confused. I do long to continue serving God. But I did not have an easy time adjusting to convent life and oft found myself in trouble."

"What kind of trouble?"

She hesitated.

I slid a sideways glance at her to find her nibbling at her bottom lip—a full and rosy lip. As if controlled by a will that wasn't my own, my gaze traveled around her face, taking in every detail of the beauty the wimple had previously covered—her delicate ears, the long stretch of neck, the elegant collar bones.

"Must I tell you the worst parts about me during our first conversation?"

"'Tis for the best."

"You are right." She released a sigh, again drawing my attention to her mouth. "I had a difficult time maintaining the silence required in the convent. I was beaten more times than I care to admit for my transgressions."

"Beaten?" I let my knife fall idle. She'd been beaten for talking? A surge of heat formed low inside, the heat I recognized as anger, a heat that served me well in battle but would do me no good now.

She hung her head. "After three years, I had yet to learn to control my tongue, though I sincerely tried. Even now, I can hardly stay silent but a moment to allow you to take part in the discussion."

"I do not mind." I truly didn't, and I wanted her to know that whoever had beaten her was wrong. Yes, a convent might have rules of solitude and silence, but how could they justify beating someone for failing?

"Thank you, my lord. But you need not say so to be nice." She was back to twisting her fork.

"I am not nice."

Her big blue eyes rounded as though my admission wasn't what she was expecting.

Why was I becoming a bumbling idiot around this maiden? "I can be nice. But never because I am attempting to impress someone."

She studied my face.

My pulse gave a low and strange thud. What was she thinking? And why did I care what she thought of me? It didn't matter.

A moment later, she smiled. "I can see that the rumors about you are indeed true. You are a good and noble man, Torvald Wahlburg."

I didn't know why, but her words warmed me. I wanted to continue staring at her, taking in her smile. But I shifted my attention to my plate, giving myself a stern warning to maintain a wall between us. Such a barrier would be for the best, keeping us both safe and in the places we belonged.

Chapter 5

Karina

Was it possible to fall in love in one night?

I was fairly certain love couldn't develop so quickly, that all the swirling warmth inside was more infatuation than anything. Nevertheless, I couldn't deny that throughout the evening and with every passing hour, I was growing more attracted to Torvald, and he filled my thoughts at every opportunity.

I was glad he'd finally turned to me and allowed me to explain my deception earlier in the chapel. Although he never formally accepted my apology, he seemed to have put the incident behind us. We'd talked the rest of the meal and throughout the harpist concert. Mostly I was the one who did the talking, telling him about my life at the convent, the education I'd received in Latin and history, my love of serving the poor, and my skills at embroidery.

As the music concluded, I clapped along with everyone else. When Torvald rose, I stood too.

"That was very lovely." I resisted the urge to cover

my chest and neck with my hand again.

Torvald eyed the door as if trying to determine how he might escape.

The hour was growing late, but I wasn't ready for the eve to end. Truthfully, I wasn't ready for my time with Torvald to come to an end.

Ingold, the short, bald steward, was at Torvald's side before he could move. "My lord, might I suggest a walk with Lady Karina in the garden?"

Torvald started to shake his head, but at a raised brow from his steward, he halted.

"The rain has ceased, and the clouds have passed," Ingold quickly continued. "The moon is out, and the flowers are in full bloom. I have no doubt Lady Karina would enjoy such an excursion."

"It sounds absolutely delightful." I beamed at Ingold.

A scowl darkened Torvald's countenance.

My smile slipped away. "However, I do not wish to tax Lord Torvald, as I am sure he is tired from his travels and would like to rest."

"Lord Torvald isn't tired." Both of Ingold's brows rose this time. "Are you, my lord?"

Torvald hesitated. "No."

"Are you certain?" I asked. "I was tired when we arrived last night, so I shall completely understand if you would like to retire."

Torvald glanced at Ingold, who shook his head. Then stiffening his shoulders, as though resolving himself to the task, he bowed toward me. "If a walk in the gardens would delight you, my lady, then let us arrange to meet there after donning our cloaks and gloves."

It was my turn to hesitate. Torvald was making an effort to be kind and accommodating but was most definitely holding me at arm's length. Was he reluctant to marry me? Did he not find me attractive enough? Perhaps in the end, after getting to know me, he would find me lacking and cast me aside with the hope of finding a better match.

If he did so, my father would be sorely disappointed. He was counting on me to aid in his rise to prominence. This was my chance to show him I was a good daughter, an asset to him, and that I could indeed help him.

I shoved aside the confusion over my future that had been plaguing me since I'd left the convent. I needed to put my past behind me once and for all and focus on securing this union with Torvald.

"My lady?" Torvald asked. "Have you changed your mind about the walk?"

"No. I shall relish the opportunity."

He bowed his consent, then strode away, as though he couldn't leave fast enough.

I observed his proud, broad back but a moment before sighing my frustration.

Still standing at my side, Ingold was watching Torvald too. "He seems to like you, my lady."

I couldn't hold back a soft scoffing laugh. "He seems to tolerate me."

"He just needs a little encouragement to warm up to you."

"Encouragement?"

Ingold glanced around at the clusters of people remaining in the great hall. Some, like my father, were still reclining in their chairs, eating sweetmeats and conversing. Servants, too, mingled about, clearing off the tables.

"Torvald is like any man, my lady." Ingold leaned in and dropped his voice to a whisper. "He won't be able to resist if you use your beauty and womanly charms to encourage him."

My beauty and womanly charms? After my time in the convent, I wasn't well-versed on how a woman could encourage a man with her beauty and womanly charms. But I was too embarrassed to let Ingold know. Instead, I nodded. "I see." Then I excused myself and started back to my chamber.

Marta met me in the passageway, my cloak and gloves at the ready.

"How did you know—"

"Ingold." She draped the cloak about me and winked. "He told me you'll likely spend the night with Torvald."

"No, of course not." I might be naïve after my years in the convent, but I wasn't ignorant. "I refuse to share his bed until after we are wed."

Marta released a mirthful laugh. "I would expect nothing less, dearie."

"But . . ." I wiggled uncomfortably underneath my heavy cloak, holding out a hand for Marta to put on my glove.

She tugged the soft leather over my fingers. "But . . . you can share a kiss or two with him."

I gasped, the embarrassment spreading from my face all the way through my body down to my toes.

Seeing my reaction, Marta's laugh only grew louder.

"I just met him, Marta. I cannot kiss him."

"Yes, you can. You just lean in and press your lips to his."

I pictured myself leaning toward Torvald and being so bold as to touch my mouth to his. "I could never," I whispered, relieved to note that the passageway outside the great hall was nearly deserted except for another couple who stood by the stairwell doorway holding hands and whispering to each other.

"What if I hold his hand instead?" I offered.

Marta shrugged as she finished with my first glove and then started on the second. "I think a kiss will win him over more so than holding hands."

"Really?"

"Really."

Once again, I tried to imagine lifting onto my toes and kissing Torvald right on his mouth. No doubt I'd miss his lips and end up kissing his nose or chin instead. "There must be some other way to win him."

"Then you want to win him?"

"I confess. I do like him."

"I knew it." Marta's smile inched higher. We'd had a discussion earlier when she helped me don my gown and style my hair. When I'd shared my concerns and confusion over my father's desire for me to marry, Marta had declared that all it would take was one evening with Torvald for me to like him.

She'd been right. There was something about his hard, rugged façade that beckoned to a woman and dared her to break past the barriers. It was like a challenge, but one I wasn't sure I could win, although I couldn't deny I wanted to try. "So, what should I do? Besides kiss him?"

"You can do all sorts of things."

I didn't want to think about what sorts of things my maidservant wanted to suggest. "Only give me virtuous ideas, Marta." My plea was soft and filled with my embarrassment.

She fitted my last glove, then squeezed my hands. "You'll do fine, my lady. All you have to do is offer him a little encouragement."

Encouragement. The same word Ingold had used.

"Smile at him. Try to catch his eyes when you're talking. Jest with him a little. Find a way to compliment him."

"That sounds doable—"

"And if the opportunity arises, brush your arm against his, graze his hand, comb back a strand of his hair . . . or stumble and hold onto him for support."

"Oh my." I fanned my face at the thought of doing any one of those things. "I never realized gaining the attention of a man could be so complicated."

Marta pulled back just a little and studied me. "One way to make it less work on your part is to give him reason to woo you first."

"I cannot imagine him ever wanting to . . . do any of that to me."

"He will." Marta spoke with more confidence than I'd ever felt. She plucked at the pins holding my caul in place. In the next instant, she lifted the elaborate head covering away.

"What are you doing?" I grabbed for it, but she held it out of reach.

"You have incredibly gorgeous hair, and we're going to let him see that." She began to unravel one of the long coils.

"Marta, no." I tried to pull away, but she refused to release the plait. "I don't want him to see the red."

"It's copper."

"Red."

Her fingers flew over my hair until it was hanging loosely. Then she started on the second coil.

"He will take one look at my hair and have no wish for me."

"He'll take one look at it and want you more than any other."

Marta was exaggerating, and though I was tempted to gather up my hair, wind it into a tight knot, and conceal it with my hood, I let her finish. I might as well allow Torvald to behold what he was gaining in marriage to me. Why not give him a good look tonight? He'd discover the truth soon enough anyway. Even if he forced himself to go through with the wedding, at least I'd spare him the displeasure later.

"There." Marta combed her fingers through the thick waves. "You are beautiful with your hair unfettered, my lady."

"Thank you, Marta." My maidservant had always been profuse with her compliments. And while I appreciated her kindness, I never believed her.

She situated some of my hair in front and let the rest flow down my back. "Now let's go and show Torvald exactly what a special and wonderful woman you truly are."

If only it were that easy.

Chapter 6

TORVALD

I DIDN'T WANT TO TAKE A WALK IN THE GARDEN WITH LADY Karina. If only I'd had the fortitude to tell Ingold no.

I paced back and forth in front of the overgrown path that wound through the flowerbeds.

At the very least, the night was balmy, almost warm, with the frigid temperatures of winter and spring finally giving way to the warmth of the coming summer.

The bright moonlight revealed too many weeds sprouting between the cracks in the stone pathway. But thankfully, the darkness obscured the rest of the deplorable state of the gardens—the lack of pruning, the overgrowth of the shrubs, and the dead, brown plants left from the previous summer.

At the patter of nearing footsteps, I paused then drew in a deep breath. I could do this, could spend another hour with her on a walk. After all, I'd survived dinner and the concert.

In fact, the time with her had passed quickly and had even been surprisingly pleasant. She was easy to talk to and had an agreeable disposition. Not only had she apologized for the deception earlier in the chapel, but she'd seemed genuinely remorseful. Though she'd been thrust into her father's plans so suddenly, she hadn't spoken one negative word the entire time. In fact, she seemed eager to please, not only her father but also me.

It was difficult not to like her. It was also difficult not to notice how pretty she was.

This was a business arrangement. Only a business arrangement. I drilled the words into my head again.

The footsteps drew closer. Two pairs. Both light and belonging to women. Which meant Lady Karina had her maidservant with her.

I let the tension ease from my shoulders. We would have a chaperone, and I wouldn't be alone with her after all as Ingold had suggested. Before my leaving the keep, he'd cornered me, informed me that I'd be by myself with the lady. He'd admonished me to do whatever I could to win her over and had given me a grin and a wink, letting me know exactly what he had in mind.

I'd refrained from taking a swing at Ingold for his inappropriate comment. Instead, I barked at him to cease from his scheming before heading outside as fast as my feet could carry me, all the while trying to keep from thinking about how a kiss would be one way to win over Lady Karina.

In fact, kissing her would be an easy way to chase away any of her doubts that might remain. At the same time, I didn't want to take advantage of her admiration, for it had become clear throughout the meal that she regarded me with the awe that so many other maidens did.

"I have never seen so many stars out all at once." Her

reverent comment came from behind me. "'Tis truly a glorious sight."

I turned to greet her, first taking in her maidservant, who'd stopped a short distance away. From the way she was inching back, I realized Ingold had likely instructed her on the plan to leave us alone.

"Stay." My command came out sharper than I intended, so that the woman froze mid-step.

I could feel Lady Karina's eyes upon me, and I softened my tone. "I bid you stay and wait to escort Lady Karina back to her chamber when we are finished with our walk."

The maidservant curtsied.

"Thank you, Marta," Lady Karina spoke kindly.

I'd noticed the way she'd interacted with all the servants throughout the evening. She'd been considerate, humble, and grateful with each person. And I liked that immensely.

I shifted my gaze, and my body ceased functioning at the sight of her. Speechless, I could only stare at her hair cascading over her shoulders, thick and beautiful. The reddish-brown color made it as luxurious as the richest and best furs I'd ever seen.

She plucked at a strand and held it out. "Yes, 'tis red."

"'Tis . . . 'tis . . ." How could I possibly describe her hair without coming across as a sappy poet?

"It has been my nemesis for my whole life." She dropped the lock and started gathering up the rest of her hair, as though she intended to coil it up and hide it.

"Leave it." I tugged her hand away, allowing it to spill back down around her.

She stared at my hand still upon hers.

I released my hold. I was being an uncouth brute. "Please."

Her eyes widened, revealing the exquisite blue. "It does not repel you, my lord?"

"Not at all."

"Not even a little?" She combed her fingers through the waves.

Suddenly I wished I could do likewise, and I clasped my hands behind my back to keep myself in check.

"I was grateful for my wimple to cover this hideousness, and now I feel as though I should contain it."

"No. You should never cover it again." I'd seen many inspiring sights during my travels throughout Norvegia. But I'd never seen anything as majestic as Lady Karina standing in the moonlight with her red hair flaming about her pale face. I could stand there and gaze upon her all night and never tire of the sight.

"Thank you. You are being too nice."

"Remember. I am not nice." Was I flirting with her?

She smiled, and again I was left speechless at the sight of her. Somehow, I managed to extend my arm in a chivalrous offer to guide her during our walk. As she slipped her gloved fingers into the crook of my arm, her shoulder brushed my bicep, sending a jolt of awareness through me.

It was an awareness I didn't want to feel. And I was tempted to pull away and put distance between us.

"Too late," she was saying. "You have already revealed your secret to me—that you are nice."

She chattered as we walked along the stone path, stopping once in a while to examine a flower and exclaim over its beauty. She talked about the gardens back at her estate in Finnmark and how she'd missed them while living in the convent. She shared more about her childhood and family, and from everything she said, I could tell she'd been happy while growing up and loved her kin. She certainly hadn't left them to escape a difficult life. And her father hadn't seemed inclined for her to go.

"Why did you enter the convent?" I asked as we sat on a stone bench near the roses. She was no longer holding my arm, which was for the best, since I'd been entirely too conscious of her fingers tucked against me. Even though the stone bench was short, I'd kept several inches between us, nonetheless.

She tilted her head back and peered up at the sky. "I wanted to serve God."

"And . . ."

From the corner of my eye, I could see her pivot and look directly at me, just as she had in the chapel earlier. "What makes you think there is more to my answer than that? Isn't serving God sufficient?"

"Perhaps. But not with you."

A gentle breeze stirred her hair as she boldly observed me. The strands swirled as though beckoning me to stroke them.

I forced my attention up to the stars. "I do not believe you were made for the convent, my lady." The idea of her locked away in so silent a place was as sad as the thought of locking a songbird in a stone chest.

She remained quiet, as though contemplating my declaration.

A vibrant and beautiful woman like her deserved the freedom to fly and sing as well as create more beauty around her.

"I decided to enter the convent to cease being a nuisance and burden to my family." Her admission was soft.

Her honesty deserved my fullest attention. I shifted so

that I was sideways on the bench, facing her.

She traced a line of golden embroidery on her skirt, the thread seeming to glow in the darkness. "When I was nearing the age of fifteen, I was allowed to attend my first ball. I thought all was going well. Potential suitors were asking me to dance and paying me attention. When one of them invited me to join him and a few other couples in the garden, I went willingly."

I tensed, not liking the direction her tale was taking.

"While walking, he asked if he could—if he might—well, kiss me."

A strange surge of protectiveness shot through me. "I hope you did not allow it."

"No." She ducked her head. "Of course not. But he spoke the words I am sure everyone present was thinking. He told me that with my red hair, I was lucky he wanted me, that no one else would."

A low growl of protest formed in my chest. How dare any man voice such untruth? He'd likely done so to manipulate Lady Karina into giving him the kiss.

"After that night, I realized I was better suited for the convent, as I did not wish to burden my father with trying to find a match for me when the task would be so difficult." Her hair fell around her, shielding her face.

Before I contemplated what I was doing and talked myself out of it, I reached for her hair. The moment my fingers connected with the thick velvet, I wanted nothing more than to delve in deeper.

But I forced myself to think about her and the hurt she'd experienced. I parted the curtain of her hair a little further and could see that she was focused on the intricate embroidered pattern on her skirt, tracing the lines absently.

I waited for her to look up at me. When she didn't, I gently slid her hair back even further, tucking it behind her ear. In doing so, I accidentally grazed her neck.

She inhaled quickly and lifted her gaze to mine.

"That man was a fool." My voice was hard, and I tried to soften it. "The task of finding you a husband would be difficult only because your father would have too many choices."

"Do not flatter me, my lord."

I wound my fingers deeper and in the same motion spanned the distance between us, drawing our heads together so that she was but inches from me.

Her eyes rounded, her long lashes giving her an innocent look that only stirred something dangerously hot inside me.

I let my fingers become tangled and lost in her hair while I held her in place. "I never flatter." I had the overwhelming need to bend down and capture her perfect lips. They were slightly parted, and her chest rose and fell in rapid succession.

Was she just as affected by our interaction as I was?

When was the last time I'd been so near to a woman? I'd denied myself for so long that I couldn't recall feeling the kind of desire that was pumping through my blood with ever-increasing intensity.

"The reason my father has choices for me is because of his wealth."

Her words were like a slap of freezing water across my face.

"Tell me," she whispered. "Would you be willing to marry me if not for my father's offer of so large a dowry?"

Another icy blast pummeled me. I disentangled my fingers from her hair and was on my feet and facing away from her in the next second. The loathing and anger I'd kept bottled inside me pushed for release.

A part of me wanted to deny her question, to tell her she was worth more than her father's wealth. But she'd asked me to be genuine with her. Even if she hadn't requested my honesty, I could give her nothing less.

At the touch of her fingers upon my arm, I flinched.

"Forgive me." Her voice contained nothing but kindness. "My question was unfair—"

I spun and took hold of both her arms.

Again, her eyes widened.

"You deserve someone better than me."

"No." She shook her head. "I am honored you would consider me—"

"Even without your father's wealth, men would vie to have you." I wasn't proficient with speaking my feelings and thoughts, but I sensed this was one time when I needed to make sure she understood how I felt.

"Vie? Now you truly are exaggerating."

I perused her body, slowly, so that she would know exactly what I was doing. Then I met her gaze frankly, hoping she could see the appreciation in my eyes.

Chapter 7

Karina

Embarrassment rushed through me at Torvald's bold appraisal.

I'd never had a man look at me the way Torvald was. His eyes held admiration and something else I couldn't name but that made my stomach flutter just like the new blossoms tossing about in the night breeze.

"I never flatter. And I never exaggerate." His voice was low and firm.

I loved him. Yes, I truly did.

As though hearing my thoughts, he glanced up to the sky, the muscles in his jaw flexing.

Infatuation. It was only infatuation. Nevertheless, with each passing moment I spent with him, I liked him more.

"Thank you, my lord, for making me feel better about my appearance. You did not have to say anything, but instead you have gone out of your way to be sincere."

He hadn't denied he was marrying me for my dowry. And he hadn't lied to me and told me he would marry me regardless of the wealth I could bring him.

The truth was, neither one of us would be here if not for being thrust together by our circumstances. He needed my dowry. And my father needed the connections. There was no sense in ignoring the facts or pretending to have more noble aspirations.

On the other hand, regardless of what had brought us together, we could move forward and make something solid of our relationship, could we not? I was fairly certain he had every intention of following through with our marriage on the morrow. His reluctance toward me seemed to be dissipating. He hadn't been repelled by the sight of my red hair. He even seemed to like me.

I didn't understand why he'd said I deserved someone better than him, for I couldn't imagine anyone better existed.

"The hour grows late." He glanced in the direction where Marta was yet waiting on the fringe of the garden.

All of Marta's advice came rushing back—the need to smile at Torvald, catch his eyes, jest, or compliment him. I'd done very little of it. I'd done even less of the physical contact.

Yes, he'd touched my arms and hair. And he'd even grazed my neck—though I was certain that had been an accident. Each instance had left me breathless with anticipation.

Was it possible I could do the same to him? Did I need to show him more clearly that I was interested, that I wanted to win him over? If so, I needed more time to do so.

I glanced around, my mind scrambling for an excuse to linger with him longer. My attention landed upon the stable where the cows and goats were housed. During my exploration of the castle grounds earlier in the day, I'd discovered a litter of puppies there. I'd gone back several times to visit.

"Before we retire," I said, "may I show you something first?"

He hesitated, then nodded. "Of course."

I started forward, then stopped. Beginning now, I had to be intentional with Marta's suggestions. I turned and attempted to give him one of my brightest and sweetest smiles. Then I held out my hand.

His attention flicked from my smile to my hand.

What did he think? Was I being too obvious in my effort to win him? Even if I was, the deeds were done. I couldn't retract my smile or hand now. I extended my fingers, beckoning him.

A frown creased his forehead.

"I promise you will love it." I tried to make my voice light.

Several more seconds passed before he placed his hand in mine. I was still wearing my gloves and wished I'd thought to remove them first. As it was, I captured his hand, wrapping it tightly within mine before tugging him along.

"I am taking Torvald to the stables," I called to Marta. "Please do not tarry any longer on my account. I shall be fine on my own."

"Yes, my lady." She bowed her head, but not before I caught sight of her knowing grin.

"The stables?" Torvald allowed me to guide him

and didn't pull away. "What do you hope to show me there?"

I tossed him another smile over my shoulder. "You must wait, my lord. 'Tis a surprise."

He didn't smile, nor did he object.

As we neared the thatched building, a groom stepped out of a side door. "My lord." He bowed, even as he hastily finished donning what appeared to be his tunic. "How may I help you?"

Torvald halted beside me and made no move to extricate his hand from mine. "We have need of a candle."

The groom disappeared inside what was likely his living quarters before returning a moment later with a glowing light. Torvald waved him ahead of us. With a nod and a look of curiosity, the groom ducked through the low entryway into the warm darkness and the scent of damp hay.

Releasing Torvald's hand, I moved ahead into the hay mow. There, in the middle of a bed of rags, the mama dog lay sprawled out with six tiny puppies curled against her.

I dropped to my knees, divested myself of my gloves, and reached for the runt, a bundle of furry black and white. His eyes were closed in slumber, but his pink nose began to sniff the air, as if he recognized my scent. A second later, he yawned and cracked open one eye.

"Hello, little love," I whispered before pressing a kiss against the puppy's forehead.

In the next instant, Torvald was kneeling beside me.

The mama dog lifted her head and eyed the two of

us warily. Torvald held out his hand to her, letting her sniff him before he gently stroked her head.

I kissed the runt again, and this time was rewarded when his rough tongue lapped at my cheek in return. I couldn't contain my laugh of delight.

"Is he not the sweetest creature you have ever seen?" I asked as the puppy gave me several more licks.

Torvald was still petting the mama, who seemed to recognize him or perhaps find comfort in his touch, for she laid her head down and closed her eyes.

I held the puppy toward Torvald, giving him no choice but to look at it. "He is adorable. You must admit it."

Torvald didn't spare the pup a glance. "He is too small and will not survive much longer."

My delight fell away, and I sat back on my heels. "I shall do whatever I must to help him."

Torvald paused.

I reached for Torvald's hand, and this time without our gloves, my fingers grazed his.

He grew motionless, clearly as aware of my touch as I was of his.

"I believe every life is worthwhile, that every creature big or small deserves a chance."

He didn't move his hand from mine.

I willed him to look at me, and as though sensing my plea, he shifted and met my gaze. Up close, the grayish blue of his eyes was dark, almost murky. Stubble covered his jaw and chin, and I had the strangest urge to run my fingers over the scruffy layer. The thin scar on his cheek that I'd noticed earlier at dinner also summoned me to touch it.

I knew this was a moment Marta would want me to take advantage of. But I couldn't. I was suddenly too breathless and weak. This closeness was overwhelming. Everything about Torvald was overpowering me.

His attention dropped to my mouth. His nostrils flared slightly before he jerked his gaze back to the runt.

Without saying anything, he took the puppy from me. He held the runt up with one hand, examining him. The pup began to squirm and wag his little tail. An instant later, as Torvald brought him closer to check his ears, the pup managed a lick to Torvald's nose.

I laughed, the sight too precious to waste on anything but joy.

Torvald's lips twitched with the beginning of a smile.

I hadn't yet seen him smile, and I suddenly wanted that more than anything else. As one of the other puppies stirred and pushed to its wobbly feet, I picked it up and kissed its soft warm head. When it kissed me in return, I let it have its way, laughing with each lick.

As Torvald cuddled the runt against his chest, he watched me, and finally a small smile appeared. The sight was so beautiful I wanted to capture it and save it, for I guessed Torvald was not a man given to smiling or laughing or finding joy in the little things of life.

Soon all the puppies were awake and hungry. We let them nurse, then afterwards we played with them until they fell back asleep, exhausted.

I leaned against the cool wattle and daub wall, the runt curled in my skirt. Torvald sat beside me, two puppies in his lap, his strong fingers tenderly scratching behind their ears. Their little mouths almost seemed to be smiling their pleasure at his touch.

I breathed in my contentment. I could be happy like this here at Wahlburg Castle with Torvald, couldn't I?

Torvald stretched out his legs as though getting himself more comfortable. The groom had left the candle for us and now waited just outside the stable door, not seeming in a hurry.

"What will become of the puppies when they are full grown?" I asked.

"They are bred to be sheep dogs."

"That must mean you have sheep."

"Many of our tenants raise sheep. The rugged hills this close to the Snowden Range allow for little else."

For a while, we talked about the area around Wahlburg Castle, the sustenance the land provided, including the hunting, fishing, and lumber. He spoke of the peril from the Ice Men living in the nearby mountains and shared about an attack against the castle when he'd been but a boy. His father had almost single-handedly driven the Ice Men away and saved their estate.

I'd yet to meet Lord Wahlburg. Ingold had told us the elderly lord was ill of health and spent most of his time in bed. He'd even indicated the lord was deteriorating rapidly and may not have long to live.

Before I had the chance to ask Torvald about his father's health, he shared more about the Ice Men and the battles he'd faced over recent years with the fierce mountain men who claimed neither Norvegia nor neighboring Swaine as their home.

Our talk of battles led to his work as a knight for

the king, and I was thrilled to hear his recounting the tale of Ansgar and Lis meeting and falling in love. Apparently, they'd even spent a day or two at Wahlburg Castle before returning to Vordinberg and saving King Ulrik from Rasmus, a devious Royal Sage who had schemed against the previous king. Although they'd been able to free the king, eventually he'd passed away, leaving the throne to Ansgar and Lis.

When Torvald stifled a yawn, I placed the runt back with his mama and then settled the other two in the warm huddle as well. I stood and held out a hand to assist Torvald to his feet. "I have been insensitive, my lord. You are tired after a long day of traveling and should be abed."

He hesitated but a moment before placing his hand in mine.

I tugged him up, but as he climbed to his feet, the momentum threw us off balance. I fell back against the stable wall, and he stumbled into me.

I laughed at our bumbling.

He steadied himself by leaning his forearms on the wall on either side of me.

"I apologize, my lord. I am clumsy more times than not. On the way here, I fell off my horse once, tripped into a river, nearly caused my brother's horse to rear up, and—"

He brushed a strand of hair away from my face, his fingers grazing my cheek.

I became aware of the length of his body against mine. The pressure wasn't heavy or suffocating. Rather it was enticing, almost intoxicating to feel the broadness of his chest, the hardness of his muscles, the solidness of his limbs.

I had a sudden and brazen need to wrap my arms around him in an embrace.

He combed at my hair again, so gently. The echo of the touch whispered through me, almost like a thread weaving through satin, drawing me tighter.

"My lady." He let his gaze wander over my features. "I shall not marry you on the morrow if 'tis not what you wish."

In this moment, he could pick me up, carry me to the chapel, and I would marry him in the next heartbeat if he but asked. In so few hours, how had I become entirely captivated by him?

If only I didn't still sense his reluctance. Yes, he'd been polite and kind and attentive. But underneath it all, he was tense, as though he would bolt away from me and Wahlburg if he but could.

Did I yet need to do more to encourage his affection for me? Or was I simply never going to be good enough for any man?

His eyes finally connected with mine, the power of the steely gray-blue severing the air from my lungs.

"Likewise, my lord." I struggled to speak. "I shall not marry you on the morrow if 'tis not what you wish."

His face was less than a hand's span away. His expression was unreadable, as were his eyes. What was he truly thinking?

"I have never been inclined toward marriage," he said slowly, as though determined to give me an honest answer. "And I cannot promise you my heart, as I have vowed never to give it away."

Vowed never to give his heart away? What did he mean?

Before I could voice my question, he continued. "Nevertheless, if we wed, I do vow to respect and honor our arrangement and you as best I am able."

Respect and honor? What about love and cherish?

He leaned away, breaking our contact and leaving me chilled.

A swell of disappointment crowded into my chest. He was a man of such honor that he wanted me to understand the truth about marrying him—that marriage wasn't something he wanted, and he had no intention of making it more than an *arrangement*.

Essentially, he was asking me if I could live within the confines of a loveless marriage. If I couldn't, he was giving me the chance to reject him first and walk away.

A part of me wanted to tell him no and return to the convent where my heart would remain safe from the hurts and insecurities that came with relationships with men. There I could continue in unfettered devotion to God and to serving the poor. There I would be free from loving a man who was admitting he would never allow himself to love me in return.

If I left, I might protect myself and prevent heartache. But not only would I disappoint my father and deprive him of his aspirations. What if in doing so, I missed out on the opportunity to have more than I'd ever dreamed possible? What if I could eventually win Torvald over? What if I could break past the barriers imprisoning his heart?

I hesitated. I would be taking a risk by accepting his conditions. There was the chance I might pour out my love and affection upon him and never gain his in return. Could I live with that?

I'd known from the start that this was a marriage of mutual benefit and nary one of love. Why, then, after meeting Torvald, was I seeking more? Was it because he was so much more than I'd anticipated? Was it because I was so much more attracted to him than I'd expected to be?

He took a step away from me, his shoulders stiffening. "I shall not fault you for your decision—"

"Yes."

His brows lifted, and he searched my face.

Yes, I could live with the terms he was setting. But hopefully, I wouldn't need to. Hopefully, with time and patience and love, I could overcome the barriers and convince him to give me his heart.

"Regardless of your stipulations, I shall marry you on the morrow."

He expelled a tense breath.

Was he relieved I was still willing to marry him, or was he disappointed I hadn't cut our ties and freed him from this obligation?

Whatever the case, I would need to increase my efforts and do everything within my power to win him over.

Chapter 8

TORVALD

We stopped in front of Karina's chamber door. The wall sconces put out scant light in the dark passageway at the late hour. And we were alone, since the other guests as well as the servants were no longer stirring about.

After walking with her in the garden and then visiting the puppies, my attraction to her had grown, so much so that when we'd bumped into each other in the stables, I'd been tempted to throw caution aside and give in to my desire.

There was something especially tantalizing about her. Was it her wide eyes? Her delicate face and the sprinkling of freckles? Her gorgeous hair? Her sweet nature? Maybe it was everything combined, although she was too innocent to realize how much she affected me.

Whatever the case, I'd found myself falling deeper under her spell. And I'd thrown out the last defense I had left. I'd told her the truth, that I wasn't interested in developing anything between us, that I had no plans to have a heart match.

I'd watched the indecision ripple across her features. I couldn't deny that I would have been disappointed if she'd refused to marry me and told me she was leaving. 'Twas selfish of me. When she'd agreed to go along with the union even knowing how I truly felt, I'd been relieved.

But now, once again, my selfishness glared at me. I wasn't thinking about her needs or her future or how the marriage would impact her. I was only thinking of myself.

She paused in front of the door, holding the handle. Her back faced me, and I had the need to let myself gaze upon her one more time before leaving her for the night. But I crossed my arms and kept myself from touching her hair or her arm or her shoulder so that I wouldn't prolong this parting.

She hesitated a moment longer and then spun. Framed by her long lashes, her eyes were wide and guileless. Before I could think or react, she rose on her toes and brushed a soft kiss against my lips. Then just as fast, she turned, opened the door, and darted into her chamber, closing the door behind her.

I couldn't move, could only stare at the dark panel. My lips tingled, and heat swirled low in my gut.

She'd kissed me. It hadn't been long, but it had been warm and delicious, like the briefest taste of a delicacy that leaves a person wanting to partake of the entire treat.

With the sweetness of her lingering on my lips and imprinted on my mind, I craved the feast. I lifted my hand to knock, to draw her back, so that I could take a full kiss, this one longer and more thorough.

But what good could come of such intimacy? It would only erode my defenses all the more.

With a shake of my head, I pivoted and forced my feet

to lead me away. I retired to my chambers, hoping I could slumber and put Karina from my mind. But I only tossed and turned upon my bed. Finally, frustrated with myself for thinking of her so much, I arose and headed to the antechamber behind the great hall where my father and Ingold kept the ledgers.

I'd never taken the time during any of my other trips home over the years to inspect the financial records. But it was past time for me to do so. With the coffers nearly empty, I needed to discover what was draining our resources and come up with a solution.

After gathering the leather binders containing the ledgers from the past ten years, I stacked them on the writing table, sat in my father's chair, and began reading them. By the time the first light of dawn stole into the room, a strange troubling plagued me. Something wasn't right with the ledgers. The columns weren't adding up. But I couldn't figure out why.

Some of the entries from previous years were written in my father's sloppy penmanship. But most were Ingold's. He'd kept meticulous records of each item bought and each coin spent in every area of the estate. He'd even marked the donations to churches, abbeys, and the poor.

I arose with a stretch, guessing I ought to rest for a few hours before my nuptials. As I wound through the great hall, I glimpsed a spot of red hair as I crossed by a passageway. Karina? I halted, then stepped back and peered down the long corridor.

Yes, there she was at the end, whispering with someone at the side door of the keep.

She hadn't slept long after our late night together.

I hesitated to disturb her. After all, she didn't need

someone hovering over her and making her feel as though she wasn't trustworthy. Because she was trustworthy, wasn't she?

I hovered out of sight and watched her a moment more. When she disappeared outside as though readying to leave, my heart began to thud. What was she doing and where was she going at so early an hour?

A sharp angst pushed me down the hallway. With each step, the angst prodded harder, until my chest hurt. By the time I reached the end, my footsteps thudded loudly. I threw open the door, not caring that it banged against the stone wall of the keep.

Standing at the end of a wagon nearby, Karina jumped and let out a startled gasp.

With a scowl I didn't try to wipe away, I strode past several kitchen staff and approached Karina. "What business are you about?" My tone was laced with accusation.

Her hands fluttered to her chest, and she clutched at her cloak. "My lord, I did not expect you to be awake at this hour."

"So you intend to sneak around while I sleep?"

"Sneak around?" She bumped against the wagon in her effort to put distance between us, but I was too quick and boxed her in, giving her no way to escape.

"You are engaging in clandestine activities and thought I would not discover them."

"'Tis not the case at all." Her eyes were wide, as if I had indeed caught her in the middle of something she shouldn't be doing.

I grabbed her arm. And though I wanted to shake her, I held my anger in check. But barely.

The servants around us were slipping out of sight

through the side door, all except the groom who had served us when we'd visited the puppies. He stood in front of the mule hitched to the wagon and eyed me warily, his hands fisted at his sides.

The inner bailey was quiet, but I could see the stirrings within the various buildings, and erelong, everyone would be bustling about.

"My lady?" The groom focused on Karina and then on my grip upon her arm. "Do you need my assistance?"

"Thank you. I am just fine."

"You're sure?" The man drew up his spindly shoulders. "I'm stronger than I look and can defend you." As he spoke his bold words, he aimed them at me.

"You are too kind, James." She offered him a smile. "But I am in no danger. I assure you."

I glanced from Karina to the groom. "How do you know his name?" My question was again accusatory.

"I asked him."

He was a middle-aged man who'd taken over the position long after I'd left to begin my knight training. I'd seen him from time to time during visits, but I had no knowledge of his name. I honestly hadn't ever paid him much heed. Now as I took him in, I beheld kindness in his leathery brown face. The way he was looking at Karina was fatherly. Nothing about him suggested he had other aspirations toward her.

And Karina?

I studied her face. The delicate lines, pale skin, and natural beauty were haloed in faint morning light. How could she look so innocent if she was doing something amiss? Had I overreacted?

"I beg your forgiveness, my lord." She examined my face with equal measure. "I should have asked you, too, before embarking on my mission this morn."

"What mission?" I loosened my hold on her arm but didn't release her.

She tilted her head toward the back of the wagon. "I spoke with your father, Lord Wahlburg, and he gave me his blessing."

"You spoke with my father?" This woman was confounding me more by the second.

"Yes, I went to his chamber already this morn and asked him if I might distribute the leftovers from the feast last night amongst the poor."

For the first time since stepping outside, I glanced at the contents within the wagon bed. There were several covered cauldrons, crocks, a crate of bread, and more. For the first time, I also noticed her attire. She wore a brown cloak that covered her garments—a cloak that was so simple and plain, I guessed she'd brought it from the convent. She certainly wasn't dressed to impress anyone. If anything, she was downplaying her beauty.

"While journeying here," she said, "I noticed a village just north and west of the river, not far from Wahlburg. It appeared as though it has suffered greatly in recent years. So I asked James if we could take the food there, and he has graciously agreed to accompany me."

I knew of the village she referenced. It had been attacked by the Ice Men the previous autumn. The warriors had wrought destruction, killed livestock, and ruined crops. We'd since learned that King Canute of Swaine had hired the Ice Men to aid him in his attempted takeover of Norvegia. And with Wahlburg so close to Swaine and the Ice Men, I suspected the estate and its tenants would continue to be in danger, even more so with the fortifications in disrepair.

Karina placed a hand on my chest nigh my heart. "I pray you will give me your blessing as well."

Her touch seared through the linen tunic, reminding me I'd shed my outer garments and was not fully attired. As she grazed the spot above my heart, she focused on it, a rosy hue climbing into her cheeks. My thoughts returned to the kiss she'd given me at her chamber door, and my attention dropped to her lips, those soft lips that had brushed mine only hours ago.

"What say you, my lord?"

I took in the situation again, and this time I saw it for what it was. Karina had requested help distributing the food. The groom had come to her aid. In fact, he'd even offered to defend her against me. He was a gallant man—albeit foolhardy—to think he could fight me off. He surely knew I was an experienced warrior, one of the best in the land.

I met his gaze. "I am grateful for your loyalty to Lady Karina." I hoped he understood that was as much of an apology as I would give him.

He nodded. "'Tis easy to see she is a treasure, my lord. And I would defend her to the death."

I liked this old servant. How had I visited for so many years and never noticed his kindness? Was it because I'd always been too consumed with my own problems and pain? Or perhaps with Karina's easy love and acceptance of everyone—even the servants—she was setting an example of how to treat others that I would do well to emulate?

"Do you have time to distribute the food yourself?" I asked her. "Do you not have preparations to make for the wedding?"

"'Tis why I am leaving so early, that I might return well

ahead of the ceremony."

I owed Karina an apology too, not only from last night but now. I'd been quick to judge her by the sins of my mother. And that wasn't fair. I swiped Karina's hand from my chest, lifted it to my lips, and kissed the back of her hand.

Her fingers trembled within mine.

"I shall go with you."

Her lips curved up, and the smile moved into her eyes, brightening them. "'Tis not necessary, my lord."

Though I was tired from staying up all night, I was also accustomed to going extended periods without sleep. "My squires or I must escort you for your protection."

Her smile dimmed. "Very well, my lord." She extricated her hand from mine and then turned her attention to the back of the wagon, gathering hay around the food items to cushion them.

Had I said something wrong? Did she think the only reason I wanted to go with her was for her safety? Perhaps I needed to be clearer that I'd been jealous, that I hadn't liked the idea of her going off with another man.

I approached her from behind and then reached past her to straighten one of the crocks. My chest brushed against her back, and I felt her quick intake.

I leaned in and spoke near her ear. "I would it be me who accompanies you before my squires or any other man."

She drew in another breath. "I would that it be you too, my lord."

Her hair was coiled today, revealing her neck. The smooth stretch tantalized me with the need to bend closer and brush a kiss there. But after setting the boundary with our relationship last eve, I couldn't lead her on today to believe more could exist between us. I had to be careful so that I didn't end up hurting her.

I backed away, gave instructions to James to ready our mounts, then I returned inside to don the rest of my garments as well as my chain mail. Before the sun had fully risen, we were on our way.

We followed the river, which was swollen with the snowmelt from the Snowden Mountains. The morn was pleasant for late April, and the green of the leaves and grass seemed more vibrant, the sunshine brighter, the sky a perfect blue. Was this also because of Karina?

She kept up a steady conversation during our ride, telling me more about the charity work she'd done before going into the convent as well as the many ways she'd served the poor during her time as a postulant.

We reached the village in less than an hour. As she shared the food with the residents, she was humble and gracious, and the people fell in love with her immediately. James and I assisted her, and all too soon we were on our way back to the castle. I found myself guiding my mount slower, not ready to bring our time together to a close.

One thing was becoming all too clear—Lady Karina was easy to fall in love with. I just couldn't allow myself to do so.

Chapter 9

TORVALD

THIS WAS TRULY HAPPENING. I WAS GETTING MARRIED.

From my position nigh the altar, I watched the door, my pulse tripping in a strange rhythm as I waited for Karina to arrive. Her kin had already gathered, and they were quietly conversing on the benches. My squires stood at the back of the chapel, acting as my witnesses. And the priest waited nearby.

As the door opened, my muscles tightened.

At the sight of a manservant on either side of my father, holding him upright, surprise shot through me. I hadn't expected him to get out of bed and attend the wedding ceremony, and for a moment, I could only stare at the man who'd once been my hero—a hulking knight with strength and valor and purpose, who'd now been reduced to skin and bones . . . because of a woman.

Bitterness rose to the back of my mouth, but I forced myself down the aisle toward him. Upon reaching him, I bowed my head. "Greetings, Father."

"Torvald." His voice was raspy, but his eyes were

bright today, clearer than I'd seen them in a long time. "Thank you for being a dutiful son."

I pinched my lips together to keep from saying something rude, and instead, I nodded.

Behind my father, the door opened again, and this time Karina entered with her maidservant Marta at her side. She wore a flowing white gown that glowed with gold. Her hair was loose but contained small plaits woven with golden ribbons.

She was stunning, and my heartbeat halted altogether.

As she paused and drew in a breath, her eyes caught mine. Anxiety churned through the blue, and it was clear she was having second thoughts about going through with the wedding. I could admit, all throughout my grooming I'd waged an inner debate about whether to push forward with the nuptials too.

I'd meant what I'd said last eve. I wouldn't marry her if she didn't want the union. I lifted a brow, hoping she could read the assurance in my eyes that we need not do this if she was hesitant.

She held my gaze as though drawing strength from me and then stepped up to my father, who had also shifted to look at her. "Lord Wahlburg, I am delighted you will be able to attend our wedding after all."

Father's face filled with what I could only describe as reverence as he took in Karina. "You look lovely."

"My lord, you are so kind."

"No, my dear, you are the kind one."

Karina touched his arm. "I am heartily glad to be gaining a new father like you. I will now be doubly blessed." She held her hand out to Lord Royse, who had arisen from his bench and approached her. He returned her smile, his expression one of both love and adoration.

Ingold had informed me that Lord Royse was accustomed to giving in to the whims of his daughter. But the more I was around Karina, the more I was beginning to see that she wasn't capable of manipulating anyone. She won people over because of her sweet nature alone.

"We are blessed" my father said, leaning heavily on his manservants, "to be gaining you into our family. Is that not right, Torvald?"

"Indeed." The groom's words from earlier in the morn resounded through my head: *'Tis easy to see she is a treasure.* 'Twas also becoming clear that the only reason she had remained available for me was because she'd been hidden away in a convent until three days ago. If she'd led a normal life and mingled among the nobility like other maidens her age, another man would have snatched her up long ago—a better man, someone more deserving of a woman like her.

Karina's smile now encompassed not only her father, but all of us. The worry upon her face from moments ago was gone.

As everyone else sat down, I held out my arm toward her, inviting her to take hold, not only of me but of a new life together. Without hesitation, she slipped her hand into the crook of my arm, and together we walked to the front of the chapel and stood before the priest.

Although I couldn't extinguish the alarm bells altogether at the back of my mind—the bells that warned me against marriage—I resolved for today to try to be worthy of her.

The ceremony went quickly. We recited our vows. The priest read Scripture and prayed. I gave her a ring that had been among her mother's possessions, one her father had brought along for the occasion.

Then the priest issued a formal declaration: "As much as Lord Torvald and Lady Karina have consented together in holy wedlock and have witnessed the same before God and this company, and thereto have given and pledged their troth and have declared the same by giving and receiving a ring, and by joining of hands, I pronounce that they be man and wife together. In the name of the Father, of the Son, and of the Holy Ghost. Amen."

I murmured "Amen" just as Karina did.

I'd focused on the priest for most of the ceremony. But now, I gave myself the pleasure of looking at her upturned face, at the gentle smile upon her lips . . . the lips that had touched mine last eve.

"You must seal the union with a kiss," Lord Royse called in his boisterous manner.

A kiss? And why should we not kiss? We were married in the sight of God and man. Besides, what harm could come from a kiss? After all, Karina's brief one last night hadn't changed anything between us.

Karina's cheeks flushed. As others in her family echoed the request, she peered up at me with wide-eyed embarrassment. "I apologize, my lord," she whispered. "I know how you feel—"

I cut her off by bending in and swiftly seizing her lips. Unable to do anything only halfway, I claimed her as thoroughly and powerfully as I did everything else.

Beneath the pressure of my lips, she hesitated, and I guessed this was likely her first kiss—not including the one from last night, which had hardly counted. She truly was innocent, and that thought fueled my desire for her all the more so that I couldn't keep from deepening the kiss. As I did so, she kissed me back, rising into me and melding her mouth so perfectly with mine, I almost lost myself in her.

But at the giggles and laughter from those watching us, I broke away.

I didn't immediately put distance between us, and instead took my fill of admiring her swollen lips, reliving the feel and taste of them. How long did I have to wait before kissing her again?

The thought dragged me back to reality. I couldn't kiss her again like that. It was too dangerous. With how weak and vulnerable I was feeling at this very moment, how much weaker would I grow if I gave in to more intimacy?

Her gaze stayed fixed upon my lips, however. And they were filled with wonder, as if she'd been completely and unexpectedly swept away by the kiss.

A surge of longing rocked through me, making me want to capture her mouth again, proving to us both that the kiss wasn't a coincidence, that another kiss would be just as captivating. But if I kissed her twice, it would turn into three times, then four. And where would it stop?

I took a step back and held out my arm.

With trembling fingers, she took the offering. As her hand settled against me, my heart quavered. This woman was now my wife. My wife.

What in the name of heaven had I done?

Chapter 10

Karina

My wedding day. I pinched myself through the layers of my gown. Was I only dreaming? Would I awaken to find myself alone in my barren convent cell? I hoped I wouldn't.

The feasting had lasted for hours, and now the servants had pushed the trestle tables against the walls, making room for dancing. As the music started, I glanced at Torvald seated beside me. I'd been taking my cues from him all evening, unsure what was expected of me.

He was reclining in his chair, a goblet in one hand, seeming to be at ease. Something had shifted in me since his kiss after the wedding ceremony, something I didn't understand but that had wrought a strange sparking within me, a crackling that fanned hotter every time he looked at me.

Ingold approached from behind us. "My lord, time to dance with your bride."

Torvald nodded and then stood. Ever since we'd

been sitting side by side for most of the meal, he hadn't looked at me oft, only casting me glances from time to time. But now, as I stood, his gaze slid over me, and his eyes flashed with an appreciation that only made my insides swirl into their own dance.

He led me from the dais into the open area, and with the grace and poise that came from training, he executed the steps of the dance perfectly. With his bold gaze still upon me, I followed along, relieved I still remembered the footwork after not having danced once over the past three years in the convent.

As we moved, I was much too conscious of his strong hands, one at my waist and the other holding my hand. Every press and graze of his fingers was more than my senses could handle, so that halfway through the dance, I felt as though I might overheat from the contact. I had to distract myself somehow. "What was it like to dance with the Princess Elinor at her coming-of-age ball?"

He gave a slight shrug of his broad shoulders, which only drew my attention to the way his cote fit snuggly. I was also fascinated with the golden pin in the likeness of the Sword of the Magi clasped near his collar, signifying his participation in the Knights of Brethren. He'd been wearing it yesterday when he arrived, but I hadn't seen it since.

"You must have been thrilled to be with her."

"'Twas just a dance."

"Just a dance?" I couldn't keep from laughing. "We heard rumors that you were the favored amongst the noblemen to win her heart."

"Favored?" His expression, as usual, was unreadable. Even groomed in his finest, he maintained a ruggedness about him that was strangely appealing.

"Many of the other postulants were hoping you would win."

"You were not amongst them?"

"I did not know you and could not make such a decision."

"Now that you know me, would you favor me to win?"

"Of course not, my lord."

He cocked a brow.

"If she had chosen you, then you would not be here with me right now." The words slipped out before I had the chance to censure them. In the next instant, I could feel the heat moving into my cheeks. I focused on his chest at my eye level.

He was silent for several turns. Then as the music slowed, he tugged me closer, settling his hands at the small of my back. With my head tucked under his chin, I expelled a breath and attempted to release the strange tension that only made me want to wrap my arms around his neck and pull him into another kiss.

"I am also glad I did not win," he said softly by my ear.

"You are?"

"I would be here with you now and no other place."

His quiet declaration settled within me and filled me with a sweet sense of joy. "Verily?"

"Verily."

I pulled back and smiled up at him. Was I winning him over?

In the low lighting of the candelabras, his eyes smoldered a dark gray. His attention dropped to my mouth. Was he thinking about the kiss he'd given me earlier? I'd never known a man and a woman could kiss that way. And though I was embarrassed our families had witnessed the moment of passion between us, I couldn't deny that I would repeat such a kiss if given the chance.

Did he want to kiss me again right now?

His hand slid to the back of my neck.

My nerves tingled with sudden anticipation. But in the next instant, he gently pressed me against his chest, hiding my face from his view. I could hear the hard and fast drumming of his heartbeat. And though I was disappointed he hadn't made another effort to kiss me, I could draw comfort from the fact that my nearness was affecting him the same that his was me.

I closed my eyes, letting myself bask in the warmth of his embrace. I never would have imagined myself in this position two days ago, not even yesterday when I'd first spoken with Torvald. But somehow over the past twenty-four hours, I'd been totally and completely enriched by him.

He was everything I'd never known I wanted or needed. And I would spend my life showing him that I could be everything he'd never known he wanted or needed too.

The dancing lasted several more hours. A few times, Torvald sat out, especially while I participated in some of the folk dances. All the while I twirled and laughed and clapped with the others, I could feel him watching my every move.

I was always breathless and ready to return to his arms, loving the almost possessive way he drew me back to him.

When the dancing came to a close, I hoped Torvald would suggest another walk in the garden. I considered bringing up the possibility of visiting the puppies again, but when several of the ladies came to my side and began to lead me away with wide smiles, I grasped that this night would be very different than any other.

As the ladies and my servants helped me prepare for bed, my nerves quivered. I couldn't stop talking. And I ended up not only dropping and shattering a bottle of perfume, but I ripped a large hole in one of my nightgowns. After assisting me into bed and tucking me under the covers, they spoke blessings over me before departing.

With but one candle still lit upon the bedside table, I waited stiffly, resigned to what must be but still nervous.

The minutes passed with no sign of him, and I began to relax. I even closed my eyes and allowed myself to rest. I must have fallen asleep, because at some point I awoke with a start. The room was dark, the candle snuffed. Even so, I could see Torvald's outline as he knelt in the rushes.

"Torvald, you need not slumber on the floor."

At my drowsy whisper, he froze.

I pushed up to my elbows. "I was dozing but now am awake." As soon as the words were out, I squirmed. Should I have said anything at all? Maybe I could have continued sleeping.

He didn't move, but tension radiated through the darkness. Was he as nervous about being together as I was? I hadn't considered how he might be feeling.

"Since we have just met," he whispered, "I suggest we postpone . . . wait . . . and spend more time getting to know one another first."

Relief wafted through me, and I sagged against the mattress. "I understand . . . and I think it is a wise idea."

After a moment more, he finished lowering himself to the floor, stretching out so that his broad back faced me.

"Torvald?"

He didn't reply, but from the slight tilt of his head toward me, I guessed he was waiting for me to proceed.

"Even if we plan to wait . . ." I could feel myself blushing and couldn't force myself to speak about marital intimacies. "The bed is big enough for both of us."

The idea of him crawling in beside me was slightly intimidating. And it only made me think of the way his hands had felt upon me during the dancing. Even so, I couldn't allow my novel feelings to stand in the way of basic decency.

"'Tis not fair in the least to relegate you to the floor while I lie in comfort on the bed."

"I shall be fine." His whisper was clipped.

"No, Torvald. I insist." I scooted away from the edge. "Please. You must sleep in the bed."

He gave a low growl but didn't move. "If I get in the bed, I will not sleep. You can be assured of that." The desire in his tone was unmistakable.

I ceased my movements. Lying on my back, I stared up at the canopy.

Warmth began to thrum through my veins.

Torvald desired me. But he was being honorable and respectful of our budding relationship. At least, I hoped his resistance was because of that and not as a result of putting obstacles around his heart.

Either way, I would do my best to get to know him better and spend quality time with him over the coming days. I was determined more than ever to win him. And I fervently prayed I would succeed.

Chapter 11

TORVALD

"THE LEDGERS ARE WELL-DETAILED," LORD ROYSE ANNOUNCED from where he sat at the writing table.

I respected Lord Royse's business advice more than I thought I would. He was astute and shrewd, and his ideas for expanding our flocks and wool production were inventive. Thus, I'd invited him into my antechamber to see if he could find the problems with the Wahlburg finances that eluded me.

Lord Royse pushed away the leather-bound book he'd been studying.

Sitting across from him, I took a swig of ale, letting it cool me in the lingering late-afternoon warmth. As April passed into May, the past week had brought more spring-like weather. The open shutters of the antechamber revealed bright sunshine amidst a cloudless sky—a blue so beautiful and brilliant it rivaled the color of Karina's eyes.

At the thought of looking into her eyes during the upcoming eve, my pulse quickened. Even though I'd parted ways with her only a short while ago, I already missed her presence and wasn't sure I could wait until the supper hour to be with her again.

I'd never admit my desire for her to anyone—hardly wanted to admit it to myself. But ever since the wedding close to two weeks ago, I'd spent nearly every waking moment with her and never tired of her company.

Ingold had arranged for activities to impress the Royses. The days had been scheduled with hunting, hawking, sword-drilling, and even a jousting tournament. The evenings had contained more feasting and dancing and concerts.

In addition, I'd ridden out with Karina each morn that she delivered the leftover food to the poor. Once, on the way back, she'd convinced me to pick berries with her. Several times, she'd tugged me into the stables to visit the puppies again. Yet another, she'd pleaded with me to join her at my father's bedside, where apparently she visited oft.

The days passed much too quickly. But the nights dragged on, slowly, almost torturously so. I'd only spent our wedding night in her chamber and only so that I didn't cause gossip surrounding the validity of our union. Even though I'd considered the possibility of visiting her room and sleeping on the floor again to keep up appearances, I held back.

Being together like that had been fraught with too many temptations. The sight of her in the big bed, the sleepiness of her voice, the invitation to lie beside her . . . it had stirred up desires I didn't want to feel, desires I wouldn't be able to resist the next time I went into her chamber. I meant what I'd said about taking the time to get to know one another. And though I couldn't hold off sharing a bed with her indefinitely, I wasn't a brute and refused to use her.

The trouble was, with each passing day, I was beginning to dread leaving her and returning to Romsdal. But I'd told Gunnar upon my departure from Likness Castle that I wouldn't be gone for more than a fortnight. The two weeks was coming to an end, which meant I needed to be on my way in but a few days.

I wasn't sure how much longer the search for the sacred chalice would take, but I was determined to see the mission completed no matter the duration. I couldn't let my personal life interfere, couldn't let my thoughts of Karina deter me from my duties.

Maybe I had to try harder to guard against growing too close to her. I had to make sure that, in spite of the undeniable attraction, I wouldn't turn into the same weak-willed, lovesick man as my father. When the time came for me to ride away, I would do it.

Lord Royse was watching my face carefully. Could he see the direction of my thoughts? He rubbed at his red beard before waving his hand at Ingold, who'd been present during the several meetings I'd had with Lord Royse to garner his opinion on the ledgers, to evaluate the incoming revenue as well as the outgoing expenses. "Ingold, would you please fetch me a mug of ale?"

The steward bowed his head, but not before I caught sight of the irritation in his features. Ingold didn't like being treated like a manservant instead of the revered steward, a position of honor in the household. Yet how could he refuse Lord Royse?

He exited the room, leaving the door open in his wake.

A slight breath of air blew through the stale chamber, and it seemed to prod me to get up and find Karina. At this hour of the day, so close to Vespers, she was likely in the chapel praying. I'd learned her patterns of prayers similar to those at her convent and had gone with her on occasion. Spending time in the dimly lit chapel and kneeling at her side was one of my favorite activities.

"Let me speak frankly now that Ingold is gone." Lord Royse leaned closer. "Your ledgers cannot be accurate. With the amount of wool you bring in, you are surely making more than is listed. And your expenditures cannot be so high. Not with the deteriorating condition of your estate."

I knew he was right. I'd suspected as much myself.

"Forgive me for stating the circumstances so bluntly." Lord Royse spoke with a candor I appreciated.

"I give you leave to do so."

"Very well. I am prepared to enter into trade negotiations with you. I am looking to expand my golden textiles to include not only linen but also wool. I will pay you handsomely to give me a steady supply of wool."

I sat straighter. This was exactly the solution I needed to assist in the ongoing development of my estate and lands.

"But I cannot initiate such an agreement until you expose the source of your inconsistencies."

"I understand."

Before I could ask him what he thought might be causing such discrepancies, a knock sounded against the doorframe. One of my squires stepped through. "I am sorry to disturb you, my lord. But you have a missive from Sir Gunnar."

My pulse gave a swift kick, pushing me up from my chair. If Gunnar was sending me a message, something must have happened in the search for the chalice. It had to be urgent for him to go to the trouble. Otherwise, he'd wait until I returned.

I took the parchment, broke the seal, and flipped it open to find a message hastily scrawled. It didn't take me long to read. Gunnar had discovered the chalice was hidden with the jotunn, the creature who lived in Hardanger Forest in Romsdal. And Gunnar intended to go into the forest to seek it without me. He'd learned that Rasmus was also aware of the location of the chalice and was working to find it first.

Alarm speared me.

No one who went into the forest ever came out alive. And if Gunnar had been foolish enough to enter without any help, then he'd likely already been ensnared, perhaps even perished.

If he was languishing there, did I still have time to go in after him and help him escape? Maybe if I left right away and rode through the night without stopping, I'd be able to come to his aid.

My squire was waiting, likely sensing the message was important.

"Pack our belongings," I commanded. "We shall leave for Romsdal within the hour."

My squire nodded, then rushed off to do my bidding.

"So, your duties for the king must take you away already?" Lord Royse stood.

I folded the letter and tucked it into my vest. Then I began stacking the ledgers. "I regret I must leave you . . . and Karina so soon. But one of my fellow knights is in grave danger."

"Sir Gunnar?"

I didn't reply.

"Everyone knows that you and Sir Gunnar are searching for the sacred chalice on behalf of the king."

"Yes." Though our mission had started as clandestine, word had apparently spread all the way to Finnmark. Hopefully no one knew the true reason why the king was after the chalice, namely that it was believed to bring healing to those who drank from it.

Lord Royse rested his hands on his protruding belly. "Everyone I have spoken to believes the king is seeking the chalice because it has some sort of power to aid in defeating King Canute of Swaine just like the Sword of the Magi."

The Sword of the Magi was another sacred relic that Norvegia had protected and cherished for centuries. The king had already experienced the power of the sword last autumn. But he'd yet to test the sword in battle to determine if the legend about its ability to help the bearer defeat his enemies was true.

Was Lord Royse's assumption right? In addition to the ability to heal, did the chalice also have some sort of power in battle too?

Maybe Rasmus was aware of the powers. Or perhaps Rasmus hoped to find the chalice first so that he could bargain with King Ansgar. Perhaps he believed King Ansgar would sacrifice his kingship to King Canute in order to gain the chalice and save Lis.

Was there a risk that King Ansgar could do such a thing? He loved Queen Lis beyond anything or anyone else. Sometimes, in fact, I'd secretly groused that his love had turned him into a weakling. It hadn't made him as weak as my father, but his devotion to the queen had changed him.

Lord Royse watched me, waiting for me to confirm or deny his suspicions about the chalice.

I kept my features from revealing anything. As much

as I'd begun to like Lord Royse, I wasn't at liberty to share anything with him about the chalice. "I would that you take Lady Karina home with you to Finnmark during my absence."

"But we've only been here a fortnight." Was this Lord Royse's attempt to remind me of my part of the marriage bargain, the part where I'd agreed to help him gain popularity as a result of the marriage?

"I vow I shall fulfill my part of the deal. I shall make sure word is spread of my marriage to Lady Karina so that all the nobility throughout Norvegia knows of our connection."

Lord Royse studied me with his kindly eyes. "Even though this is an arranged marriage, I would like to see Karina happy, and so far, I believe you are making her happy."

I wanted Karina to be happy too. For as giving and loving and sweet as she was, she deserved a lifetime of happiness. But I feared if she cared too deeply for me, I would only bring her heartache.

"If Karina is happy here at Wahlburg," Lord Royse continued, "my family and I will stay with her a short while longer. The extra time will allow me to observe your sheep, the shepherds, and the shearing process more closely. Hopefully by then you will be finished and able to return to Karina."

"None of you will stay." I glanced again out the window to gauge the remainder of daylight left. I needed to be on my way soon.

"I do not mind—"

"I do not want her—any of you—here without me and my men to protect you should the Ice Men decide to attack again." Though the fortress was in disrepair, I doubted it would crumble under an attack. But I'd rest easier knowing they were well away from any danger.

Lord Royse shuddered then looked around as if he expected the Ice Men to climb in through the windows at any moment. Obviously, he'd heard tales of the fierce warriors.

"Promise you will take Karina away from here just as soon as you can make your travel arrangements?"

Lord Royse hesitated but then lowered his head in acquiescence. "Very well. We shall be on our way by week's end."

"Please, whatever you do, keep her safe." My voice was tinged with a desperation that embarrassed me.

The desperation seemed to please Lord Royse, for he smiled at me warmly. "I assure you I will do my best."

I nodded, then spun on my heels and exited. Before I left Wahlburg, I must do one last thing—I needed to see Karina and bid her farewell. I wouldn't be able to leave until I did.

Chapter
12

Karina

My heart overflowed with thanksgiving as I lifted my prayers heavenward. The castle chapel was drafty and musty, but it had become a precious sanctuary for my prayer time. It was like everything else that had happened over the past two weeks—not what I'd expected but somehow better.

Though I'd anticipated missing the convent and my life there, I truly hadn't. Yes, I missed the women I'd grown to care about. But I was finding ways to serve God here at Wahlburg.

At the opening of the chapel door, I paused in my prayers. As the heavy, determined footsteps echoed against the stone walls, my heart picked up tempo. Torvald. Only he walked with such purpose.

His footsteps halted at the front prayer rail beside me, and he lowered himself to his knees and bowed his head. His profile was etched with strength, and the dark stubble on his jaw and cheek seemed to beckon to me. I was tempted to reach out and let my fingers glide over the scruff, but I kept my hands firmly clasped together.

He was quiet for several moments before cracking open one eye and peeking at me.

I smiled, not caring that he'd caught me looking.

He resumed his prayer, bowing his head lower.

I took that as my cue to continue my silent admiration. With every passing day, I was more amazed that this incredibly handsome man was my husband. And that he wanted to be near me.

I suspected most other noblemen wouldn't have spent the majority of their leisure time with a woman. Even now, his seeking me out in the chapel to pray hadn't been necessary. But I loved every second we had together. In fact, it only made me want to be with him more.

I was learning that, though he radiated a hard and reserved façade, underneath he was sensitive and felt things deeply.

"By your staring at me, am I to assume you are done with your prayers, my lady?" he asked without breaking his prayerful posture.

"What if I am praying for you whenever I stare?" I was suddenly breathless with the joy of having him here and engaging in banter.

"Then you must be praying for me a great deal."

I laughed lightly. "Perhaps I am."

He lifted his head, his eyes open now, his gaze fully upon me. Although his smiles were rare, his lips quirked up on one side, a move I'd realized signaled his humor.

"With all my prayers, you will be the most blessed man to live."

"With all the flattery, perhaps I will turn into the proudest man to live."

"If pride were your vice, then you would already be the proudest man, since women throughout the kingdom have been flattering you for years."

"I have never paid heed to flattery."

"None at all?"

"None."

After countless activities and getting to know him, I'd grown more comfortable, and my tongue had loosened. Yes, I had already been talkative, but now I was having an even harder time holding anything back.

I sidled closer and squeezed his rigid bicep. "If I were to flatter you by saying that you are strong and muscular, would you become proud?"

His gaze dropped to my hand. "No."

We'd only had the barest of physical contact, mostly while dancing or walking or his occasional assistance. Though brief, his touch always seemed to affect me. Just a short while ago, when he'd helped me down from my saddle, the pressure of his fingers on my hips had scorched me. I'd felt the imprint of him there ever since.

Why didn't my touch affect him the same way? Or was he just better at hiding it?

Dare I experiment to find out? I'd wanted to skim his face all week. I could do so now under the guise of bantering. Because I was still teasing him, wasn't I?

Without giving myself a chance to second-guess my motivation, I traced one finger along his jawline. The scrape of his stubble was every bit as pleasurable as I'd imagined, only more so. "If I were to flatter you by telling you what a handsome man you are, would you grow proud then?"

"No." His tone was firm, but I felt the twitch in his jaw. Did he like or dislike my touch?

I hesitated, letting my fingers hover above his cheek. Maybe I needed to take care not to push him beyond what he was ready for. After all, over the past two weeks, I'd slowly begun to win him over. He was softening toward me every day. And I didn't want to jeopardize anything.

Yet, there was nothing wrong with this teasing, was there?

Impetuously, I grazed his cheek up to his temple and then the corner of his eye. "If I were to flatter you by telling you how much I like your eyes, would I puff up your head then?"

"No."

"What about your hair?" I combed a strand off his forehead. Before I could finish completely, he captured my hand, wrapping his fingers around my wrist.

Even so, he didn't say anything and didn't seem at all bothered by my touching.

"How can you remain so composed?" I asked. "If you but lay a finger upon me, I turn into a melted puddle." The moment my confession was out, I could feel the heat stealing into my cheeks and was glad for the dimness of the chapel that hid it.

He hesitated, then slowly grazed my jawline, imitating what I'd done to him. "Does this melt you, my lady?"

"Yes, very much." I leaned into him.

He traced my cheek over to my eye. "And now?"

"Of course."

He combed back a loose strand of my hair. "And?"

"I am completely undone." My voice was breathless.

As his gaze met mine, the gray-blue pierced me with such heat, my body felt on fire. He was not only melting me but was incinerating me.

"You do not play fair, my lord," I whispered. How could any one man have so much power over any one woman at such a slight contact?

"'Tis you who do not play fair, my lady." He spoke in a ragged whisper. "I admit, your touch weakens me. But one look from you slays me."

His words rendered me speechless. I could only stare at him, a mingling of awe and desire building within me.

Still holding my hand, he lifted it to his lips and pressed a kiss against my fingers. He held the kiss, his attention riveted to my mouth as though he was recalling the kiss from our wedding day and contemplating repeating it.

If he wanted to kiss me again, I wouldn't object to it. In fact, I would welcome it.

The air between us felt suddenly thick and heavy. I wanted to lean in, wrap my arms around his neck, and feel his strength surround me in return. Up until now I felt as if I'd been asleep, waiting for him to wake me up. Now he was finally doing so, and the relationship between us was turning real and alive, no longer a dream.

In the next instant, he shut his eyes, released my hand, and pulled away. "I am leaving tonight for Romsdal."

"What?" I sat back on my heels, almost as if he'd slapped me.

He lowered his head. "Gunnar is in trouble. I must go assist him anon."

Over the course of conversations, I'd pieced together more of Torvald's recent assignment with Gunnar in looking for the sacred chalice for King Ansgar. Torvald hadn't shared why finding it was so important, but he'd mentioned he would have to finish the task.

When I'd hinted at coming with him, he'd shaken his head and said he didn't know where the search would next take him and Gunnar after they finished in Romsdal, but that he would likely need to travel many more places.

He'd indicated that once he found the chalice, he would retire from being a Knight of Brethren and return to Wahlburg. But I'd assumed we would have more time before he had to leave to complete his last mission for the king.

Upon my silence, Torvald raised his head and looked at me directly, something he rarely did. "I had intended to stay at least through the end of this week. I hope you will forgive me for leaving early." His eyes held a vulnerability I hadn't seen before.

Though his news had startled—and disappointed—me, I admired him all the more for his willingness to help a friend in need. "There is naught to forgive. You are making an honorable choice to aid Gunnar in his time of need."

He stood and assisted me to my feet. Once I was standing, he didn't release my hand. Instead, his thumb brushed a gentle caress across my skin, one that almost sent me back to my knees.

"You have been patient and kind with me, my lady.

Most women would not be so understanding."

"Do not think too highly of me. For I shall be praying selfishly the whole time that you accomplish your work swiftly and return soon."

"I will send word to you in Finnmark when the time comes." He swirled a circle on my hand.

At the warm flutters his touch awakened within me, I was almost too distracted to realize what he was saying. Was he sending me away? "Finnmark?"

"You will travel with your kin back to Finnmark and stay there."

"This is my home, and I would prefer to live here now."

"I would that you be far from the border, as I fear what King Canute of Swaine may do in the days to come."

I straightened my shoulders and extricated my hand from his. "I am strong and capable. I shall fare well enough."

"'Tis possible no trouble will befall Wahlburg. But while my men and I are gone, you will live with your father." His shoulders were rigid, his back stiff, and his expression severe, as though daring me to defy him.

During my deliveries of food to the poor, I'd witnessed the remnants of the destruction wrought by the Ice Men. The Wahlburg tenants who hadn't had time to take refuge behind the castle walls had suffered injuries and death. I'd spoken to many who'd lost a family member. "I understand the danger. But why invite me here to marry you only to send me away?"

He was silent a moment, but his eyes spoke loudly enough—he hadn't been the one to invite me. Ingold had. No doubt Torvald would have waited until he'd found the chalice or until the threat of war had diminished before taking a bride. As it was, he'd been saddled with a wife he hadn't wanted, and now he had the extra responsibility of keeping his wife safe.

Wasn't that the way of things for me? No matter where I went, I ended up being a burden. I hadn't been able to help my mother the way she'd needed, had just gotten in the way. I'd been a nuisance to my siblings. And I'd caused my father strain and worry over my future.

A secret part of me had begun to think that my marriage was the beginning of something new. I was in a place where I could finally feel important, perhaps cherished. But now Torvald was telling me I was unnecessary, and he was sending me away so that he didn't have to worry about me. Was I doomed to a life where no one ever truly wanted me? Where I was shuffled from one place to the next like a relic, only there to benefit anyone who needed me?

"Very well." I released the tension in my shoulders, letting the anger and frustration easily flow away. Such anger and frustration would do me no good, only stir up bitterness in my heart. I didn't want to part ways with Torvald disagreeably. Rather, I could send him forth amiably, kindly, and prayerfully.

Torvald remained stiff.

"All the while we are apart, I shall pray for your safety."

His eyes widened as if he hadn't expected my declaration. Perhaps he'd thought I'd protest further, defy him, or even try to coerce him.

"Truly, my lord. You will be utmost in my prayers."

"Thank you."

A strange feeling slithered through me, one warning me that if he sent me away, he might never call me back.

Before I could analyze the heaviness of the prospect, a knock sounded against the chapel door. One of Torvald's squires poked his head inside. "My lord, Sir Espen has just arrived from Vordinberg and brings the latest news."

At once Torvald's eyes lit. His expression filled with purpose, and he strode away as though he'd already forgotten about me. If I'd ever believed Torvald would be content living at Wahlburg and overseeing his lands, the thought rapidly fled. Now that he was being called back to the Knights of Brethren, he radiated with energy and excitement in a way I hadn't yet seen.

When he reached the door, he paused and nodded at me. "I may not have time to say farewell. So I shall part ways now."

I bowed my head. "Farewell."

Without another look or word, he disappeared into the hallway, leaving me alone.

I shivered, then rubbed at my arms. I'd been alone oft in my life, but on this occasion, the loneliness was different, more consuming. And I feared it had come to stay.

Chapter 13

"GUNNAR IS MARRIED?" I COULDN'T BELIEVE THE NEWS.

Espen sat across the table from me, shoveling roasted venison into his mouth. I only picked at my food, having lost my appetite altogether when Espen had explained the near-death experiences Gunnar had faced during his time in Hardanger Forest against the jotunn. And I was doing my best to tamp down my irritation that Gunnar's missive had somehow been delayed in reaching me and that I'd missed so much during my absence.

Espen and I had retired to my solar for a private meal so that we could converse about the king's business without all the guests at Wahlburg hearing us. As much as I'd wanted to leave tonight, I'd postponed the departure to give Espen a chance to rest and eat before we left at dawn.

Gunnar and Espen had always shared a love of women, enjoying the attention from ladies together. While Gunnar was lanky with dark brown hair, Espen was stocky and fairer, with lighter hair. Gunnar was from a noble family and wore his wealth and prestige like a banner. Espen, on the other hand, was from humble origins and at times lacked the grace and mannerisms of the noble class.

In spite of their differences, both of them, with their dashing ways and abundance of charm, never had any trouble attracting women.

"Aye, Gunnar was married before he returned to Vordinberg." Espen wiped the gravy from his mouth on his sleeve. "To one of the villeins, a young nursemaid."

I shook my head again, unable to digest the news. When I'd left Gunnar, I'd sensed his interest—even his love—for the maidservant, Mikaela. But I hadn't expected him to wed her. And certainly not so quickly.

It was odd, indeed, that Maxim and Ansgar had gotten married when they were involved with the Sword of the Magi. And now Gunnar and I had both wedded during our quest for the chalice. Certainly, it was only coincidence.

Espen had informed me of the current situation, that while he'd volunteered to ride to bring the news to me, the king, queen, and the rest of the Knights of Brethren along with a small army of knights had set sail for Romsdal.

Apparently, Gunnar and Mikaela had also helped his great Uncle Sven escape the control of the jotunn. Sven had once suffered facial deformities in a fire, and his family had subsequently cast him into the forest to live, considering him unworthy of taking his rightful place as the lord of Likness Castle.

Though the circumstances of Sven's life had been tragic, I was amazed he'd survived for so many years and was now assisting in strategizing the return trip into Hardanger Forest. With Sven's knowledge of the terrain and the jotunn, everyone was optimistic we could find the chalice.

"And how do we know for certain the jotunn has the chalice?" I pushed away my plate and instead reached for my mug. "Did Sven ever see it?"

"The story is that a priest brought the chalice to the forest many years ago, hoping to bargain for Sven's release. But when the chalice didn't bring the jotunn the healing he believed it would, he kept the chalice but refused to release Sven from his curse."

The more I learned of the danger, the more my frustration with Gunnar mounted. He'd acted recklessly to venture in without me and had been fortunate to make his way out alive without being cursed.

"How can any of us go in without facing the jotunn's curse?" I asked.

Espen paused with his fork halfway to his mouth. "'Twill be difficult, to be sure. But Gunnar and Sven are convinced it can be done. Sven is in the process of diagramming the safest route to the caves at the heart of the forest where the jotunn makes his home and where he believes the chalice is kept."

Was the chalice worth so much risk?

I sat back in my chair, the thought taking me by surprise. I'd searched for months without questioning the king's mission. But now that the undertaking had the potential to harm and possibly kill so many people, should we proceed? Was the king acting selfishly?

Yes, I understood King Ansgar loved his wife and wanted to do whatever he could to save her. But at what point was he taking this quest too far? I didn't know how much longer I could go along with his plans without speaking the truth—that the love of a woman was turning him into a fool.

All the more reason to leave with haste. Dawn could not come soon enough.

I reached for my reins, taking them from the old groom. In the darkness of predawn, the light from his candle cast a beam into the stable, revealing the puppies wiggling about and playing with one another. From what I could tell, the runt was still alive.

Seeing the direction of my gaze, the groom—James—gave a quick nod. "Lady Karina's been coming out and nurturing that runt every chance she has."

I wasn't surprised to hear it, and the picture of her with the pup warmed my heart.

"Anyone or anything touched by Lady Karina's love is bound to be the better for it, don't you agree, my lord?"

"Yes, indeed." I glanced to her darkened window. Since our time together in the chapel yesterday, I'd only spoken to her in passing to introduce her to Espen.

She hadn't liked my decision that she must return with her father to Finnmark. But she couldn't stay here. Not only would she be safer in the far northern city, but if anything happened to me, she would fare better living with her kin.

I'd sensed her hurt, but she'd remained kind and humble, going so far as to assure me she would pray for me. I hadn't liked that I'd hurt her and had almost told her she could do whatever made her the happiest. But I couldn't back down on decisions and let my emotions cloud my good judgment.

Espen exited the side door of the keep, a sack slung across his shoulder, no doubt extra food for our journey.

My squires were already mounted, as were Espen's

men. The gatehouse was open. And dawn tinged the eastern sky above the Snowden Mountains. We needed to be on our way.

Even so, something within me couldn't dredge up the energy I needed to mount my horse. It was as if a heavy stone was tied to each of my boots, holding me in place.

"I'm ready now," Espen said, crossing toward me and munching on what appeared to be a drumstick.

I pretended to tighten the cinch of my saddle.

Espen climbed up on his horse, gnawing at the bone all the while.

I fiddled with the stirrup.

A second later, something pinged the back of my head. As the drumstick bounced to the ground, I turned and glared at Espen. Why had he hit me with the bone?

He licked at his fingers. "Go say good-bye to your wife, you dolt. You know you want to."

My gaze darted to her window again. Was that it? Was I hoping to see her one last time before leaving? Surely I wasn't turning into a lovesick fool already.

I grabbed my pommel. I had to leave now. But even as my fingers closed around my saddle, I hesitated.

Espen chuckled. "Go on. We can wait."

My fingers stiffened around the leather, an inner war waging within me. It wasn't as if I'd grown to care about her so much that I needed a final farewell. No, I wanted to see her again to assure myself of her well-being. That was all.

Espen whacked the hindquarters of my horse, forcing the pommel from my grip. In the next instant, he shoved me with his boot.

With a growl, I pushed toward the front entrance and bounded up the steps. As I reached the door, it swung open forcefully.

"Wait," a breathless voice called even as a lithe but shapely body barreled into me.

I saw her red hair before anything else. It flowed in wild abandon over her nightgown.

I caught and steadied her, and her startled eyes met mine.

"Oh, Torvald." Her chest rose and fell rapidly.

"What ails you?" I extended her to arm's length, trying to assess her for any problems.

"I overslept. I meant to be dressed and down here by the time dawn broke so that I could see you off."

She'd wanted to see me off? At the thought, warmth pooled inside.

"I am glad you have not yet left, that I might say farewell."

"I said farewell to you already." Was that the only thing I could think to say? Couldn't I find something kinder like: *Thank you for coming to see me,* or *I wanted to say good-bye to you too?* Or what about the truth: *I could not make myself leave without a final look at you.*

"Yes, I realize you are busy and must be on your way." She glanced beyond me to the men already mounted and waiting—and watching us openly and curiously. "But I wanted to wish you well and Godspeed."

"Thank you."

She peered up at me, her eyes wide and her expression innocent. In the dimness of the entryway, with a wall sconce illuminating her, she looked like an angel come down from heaven. She radiated an ethereal beauty that I would never tire of looking at. In fact, I was loath to tear my gaze away from her even now, though I knew I needed to leave.

The breeze blew a strand of her hair across her face. I

reacted before I could stop myself, lifting my hand and gently peeling the hair back. The problem was, once I felt the silk, I couldn't let go. Instead, I dug my fingers into the thick, rich locks, winding them around my fist. My other hand snaked around behind her and drew her against me.

Then, as if I'd turned into another man altogether, I lost all control and willpower. I was helpless to do anything but bend in and take her lips captive. This woman. Karina. My wife. She tasted like warmth and sunshine and beauty and everything good. She was intoxicating. And as she pressed against me and opened up to me, I could do naught less than drink deeply.

I wasn't capable of soft and tender. Instead, my kiss contained all the emotion I couldn't speak aloud. For just an instant, I feared I might be too passionate and scare her away. But at her soft murmur of pleasure and her lips moving in equal measure with mine, I only wanted to go on tasting her.

A moment later, when her fingers dug into my cloak, as though to keep me from leaving, reality crashed against me, and I broke the kiss.

What was I doing? I'd vowed to myself that I wouldn't let our relationship go deeper, that I'd maintain a proper distance, that I wouldn't allow either of us to care too much. And here I was kissing her as if I couldn't bear to depart from her.

She clung to me, her breathing coming in soft gasps. Mine, too, was labored.

When I pried her grip away and took a step back, she leaned against the doorframe and grasped it, as though without the support she would fall to the floor. I felt wobbly too. But I straightened and tried to regain my sense of balance and perspective.

"I shall miss you, Torvald," she whispered as she let her gaze linger over my face.

I wanted to tell her I would miss her too, but I couldn't get the words out. Instead, I lifted a hand, caressed my knuckles slowly over her cheekbone down to her chin. Then I spun and jogged down the steps, needing to get away from her before I pulled her back into my arms and kissed her again.

I didn't look at Espen as I mounted, though I could feel him watching me and guessed he was grinning like a court jester. Silently, I urged my horse around and headed for the gatehouse. Though I wanted to glance over my shoulder and see if Karina was still in the doorway watching me, I forced myself to ride onward.

It wasn't until we reached the river bottoms and were galloping along the path that Espen directed his horse into step next to mine.

He didn't speak, although I guessed he wanted to know more about Karina.

I pressed my lips together, determined not to say anything about her or what he'd just witnessed.

We rode silently for several more moments before he spoke. "She's beautiful."

My mind returned to the image of her clinging to the door frame, her back pressed up against it, her knuckles white from her grip, her chest rising and falling. Heat shot through me along with the need to kiss her again. Why had I walked away without another kiss?

"I'm surprised one so beautiful has fallen for a man like you." Espen's tone was filled with teasing mirth.

"Has she fallen?" The question came out of its own volition. But once it was out, I was anxious to know. Did Karina truly care about me? Enough to stay with me forever? Or would she be like my mother, easily distracted by other men who paid her better compliments and wooed her with more charm?

"She came down to say good-bye, didn't she?" Espen said. "And holy saints, if a woman kissed me the way she was kissing you, I think I would have postponed leaving for another day or two, or a few hundred."

My muscles twitched with the need to return to her.

"I could tell she is a kind woman," Espen continued. "'Tis a treasure to find a woman who is both so comely and so caring."

He was right. 'Twas easy to see that she was kindhearted. And his declaration that Karina was a treasure echoed that of the groom.

"And of course, you are fortunate that she is wealthy enough to save your family estate."

Of course, everyone knew why I'd had to marry Karina. I ground my jaw together to keep from spewing a curse at myself for being so shallow. Even if the marriage arrangement had been mutually beneficial, I was still angry I couldn't enter into it more honorably, without having to use a woman and her wealth to save the estate.

"You are fortunate, my good man." Espen's voice hinted at a frustration I'd heard there from time to time. "You have everything you could ever want in a wife." Everything he wouldn't have. Was that what he was leaving unsaid?

As the son of a fisherman from a northern clan, Espen had no claim to wealth or titles. As a young boy he'd been brought into Kristoffer's household at Prestegard Castle in Karlstadt. The only way he'd risen to fame as a Knight of Brethren was because Kristoffer's father had seen the potential in Espen and trained him alongside Kristoffer.

When Kristoffer had gone off to war, Espen had traveled with him. In the end, Espen had proven himself worthy of becoming a Knight of Brethren and serving the king just as much as Kristoffer had. Fortunately, Kristoffer was a humble man and had accepted Espen as his equal and treated him like a brother.

Though Espen mingled among the nobility and brushed shoulders with royalty, he would never have the same marriage opportunities as the other Brethren. Even King Ansgar, though a commoner, was the son of a chieftain and held prominence over a fisherman's son.

While Espen might be popular among the women, no nobleman would ever consider him a serious match for his daughter, not without land, title, or a source of income. If Espen ever retired from his service as a Knight of Brethren, the most he could hope for was a gift from the king, perhaps a parcel of land. But it wouldn't be grand, and Espen would likely be too old by that point to take a wife and start a family.

"I cannot choose any woman I want," he said quietly, almost somberly. "But if I could, I wouldn't leave her behind. Not for a single second."

I cast a sidelong glance at Espen. Was he referring to a specific woman? One that he couldn't have but whom he longed for?

Perhaps he was right in admonishing me not to take my good fortune for granted. I'd been given the opportunity to fix Wahlburg's problems. And I'd also been given a good woman for a wife. Though I hadn't deserved either blessing, Providence had bestowed them upon me. Perhaps it was time to stop taking his gifts for granted.

Chapter 14

Karina

Torvald had been gone only one day, and already it felt like one hundred.

"I can see that you miss my son." Lord Wahlburg studied my face as he lay propped against a mound of pillows at the headboard of his bed.

I patted his boney hand. "I cannot deny it."

"You are good for him."

"He is also good for me." And I loved his kisses . . .

Heat eddied low in my belly at the memory of his farewell kiss yesterday morn. It had been earth-shattering—the power when he'd tugged me to him, the consuming pressure of his mouth against mine, the magnetism of his eyes.

I was tempted to fan my face, sure it was as flushed as it felt. But I refrained, not wanting Lord Wahlburg to know exactly how much I was thinking about Torvald. I was too embarrassed to admit that I'd thought of little else.

How would I survive weeks, maybe months of

being away from him? And how did I feel so strongly about him after being married to him only nigh to two weeks?

Did I love him? Or was this still infatuation?

Lord Wahlburg leaned his head back and closed his eyes, weariness creasing his features. I still hadn't discovered what ailed him. But he tired easily, and I never stayed overlong.

"I shall leave you, my lord, and let you rest." I started to rise, but he snagged my hand with surprising strength. Though he was frail now, his body shape and size had likely once resembled Torvald's. What had happened to change him into this shell of a man?

He tugged at my hand. "Be patient with Torvald."

"How so, my lord?"

"He has not had an easy life . . ." Lord Wahlburg opened his eyes again, and the pain in their depths was deep and heart-wrenching.

I was hungry to know more about the man I'd married. But I also didn't want to pry into issues he wasn't ready for me to know.

"Torvald lost his mother when he was but a lad of eight."

I squeezed Lord Wahlburg's hand. "I am sure her death was difficult for both of you."

He swallowed hard. "She did not die. She ran away . . . with another man."

Slowly I sat back in the bedside chair. A myriad of emotions swirled through me—shock, mortification, indignation, even despair. If I could feel so many things just hearing about the betrayal, how many more feelings had Lord Wahlburg and Torvald experienced? The agony would have been unbearable.

Was that what ailed Lord Wahlburg? Perhaps he'd suffered so much from her unfaithfulness that he'd never been able to recover. And what about Torvald? In what ways had his mother's abandonment affected him?

Although I'd never experienced their level of rejection, I'd had to face being overlooked and cast aside. And I could relate to the loneliness and hurt and unworthiness.

Lord Wahlburg's head drooped so that his chin almost rested upon his chest. "You might be wondering what is wrong with me, that my wife did not want me."

"No, my lord. I was wondering what was wrong with your wife that she gave up such a kind and loving husband."

He lifted his gaze, his expression cautious.

"She could not see the blessing she had in you and Torvald if she could forsake you to run off with another man."

He was quiet for several heartbeats. "When she said she was leaving, I tried to convince her to stay, but she would not listen to reason."

"Then she clearly did not have true love in her heart if she was not willing to forgive and rebuild."

"I have blamed myself for lacking character, for perhaps doing something wrong, for driving her away . . ."

I waited a moment for him to expound, but when he lapsed into silence, I took that as my cue to say more. "'Twould seem she is the one who lacked character for chasing after another man who was not her husband."

"Perhaps you are right." He didn't sound convinced.

"I am sorry her rejection hurt you and Torvald."

Lord Wahlburg's throat worked up and down, as though he was attempting to gain the ability to speak past his heartache.

Maybe I could help Lord Wahlburg find some healing. And perhaps I could bring joy to Torvald too. In fact, what if God had brought me to this family to bring restoration?

A knock on the door was followed by my father entering. His head was down, and he was studying one of the estate ledgers. That's all he had been doing since Torvald left yesterday—analyzing and computing data.

"Lord Wahlburg, I visited several of your top-producing sheep farms yesterday." Father approached the bed. "And they most definitely are generating more wool than is being reported."

I didn't understand much of what Father was investigating, but I was happy he'd found a way to keep himself busy while at the same time offering financial advice.

Thankfully, Lord Wahlburg seemed inclined to listen. At the very least, he and Father began to converse. And as usual, Father didn't notice my presence in the room. After several moments, I rose and made my way to the door. As I opened it, Lord Wahlburg interrupted my father. "Thank you, Karina. I would love your company again later."

"Karina?" My father's gaze alighted upon me, surprise filling his face at the sight of me. "How are you faring this morn?"

"I fare well."

But his attention was back upon the ledger, and I knew he hadn't heard me. 'Twas not that he didn't care about me or my response. This was simply the way of things.

Lord Wahlburg was studying me, and I offered him a reassuring smile before exiting.

As I made my way toward my chamber, I tossed aside the heaviness and thought on Torvald instead. Had he reached Romsdal yet? With Espen's arrival, apparently there were more developments regarding the chalice, although the two had been very secretive with their discussions. Even so, I sensed everything about the search had become more intense and dangerous.

How would I wait patiently for his return when my heart longed for him with every beat?

I'd already tried distracting myself with embroidery. Sewing the delicate and intricate patterns into clothing, tapestries, and other linens usually brought me contentment, and in the convent, the needlework had helped pass the time and ease my homesickness. Yesterday, however, I hadn't been able to concentrate and had continuously poked my fingers until I'd given up. I had the feeling today I'd only be more distracted.

Before I reached my room, Ingold came running down the hallway, his footsteps echoing loudly. "My lady, you must instruct your servant to pack your belongings immediately." He was breathing hard, and his bald head was spotted with perspiration.

I paused. "Is something amiss, Ingold?"

"A scout has just arrived for Lord Torvald, and the news is grim."

My heart began a slow tap of dread. "What news?"

"King Canute and his army are on the move. And there are rumors he has hired Dark Warriors to aid him in his fight for Norvegia's throne."

The rhythm of alarm inside me picked up speed. I didn't know anything about such Dark Warriors, but they sounded ominous.

"You and your kin must leave anon," Ingold said. "There is no time to waste."

"How long before King Canute and his army cross into Norvegia?"

"From what the messenger indicated, it may only be days."

That meant additional peril would befall Torvald. Soon he would be plunged into the midst of a battle for the kingdom. I loathed the prospect that his life would be at risk. But he was a knight of the highest rank in the kingdom, with a duty to protect the king. I could not expect him to do anything less than defend the king at all costs.

"The safest way to avoid any trouble is to ride northwest toward the coast." Ingold moved past me and opened my door. "I will send you to Romsdal, where you can take news of the invasion to Torvald and find a ship to transport you the remainder of the distance."

On the journey to Wahlburg Castle, we'd traveled by ship from Finnmark to Vordinberg. From there, we'd ridden horses on the road that followed the Blood River north. As a result, we'd been able to bring many trunks of goods and gifts, as well as my dowry.

As though sensing the direction of my thoughts, Ingold shook his head. "You must pack light, only what you can take by horseback."

We were on our way by the noon hour with naught but the most essential of our belongings. Before leaving, I pleaded with Lord Wahlburg to join us. But he insisted that we go without him, believing his weakened condition would only slow us down. Also, before setting out, I dispatched word to the surrounding tenants, calling them to take shelter within the walls of the castle. I also tasked the staff to store up provisions.

When I could delay no longer and feared my father would forget me and leave me behind, I forced myself to go. With the small retinue of armed men belonging to my father, we would not be left entirely vulnerable. Even so, we rode at a rapid pace and didn't make camp until darkness fell.

"Will we have the opportunity to visit with Torvald?" I asked my father as we partook of a meal from the provisions packed for us as well as roasted game some of the men had hunted.

My father, across the fire from me, was in the middle of speaking with several of the men and didn't hear my question.

I considered repeating it but guessed my father was too distracted to reassure his newly married daughter who was pining after her husband. Sitting on a stone beside me, Marta reached for my hand. "When we get there, he'll surely come to you."

I clasped Marta's hand in return, grateful that she was always there to listen and comfort me. "I know he will be busy with his duties for the king."

"He won't be too busy for you, my lady."

"I shall not expect any of his time." The wind howled through the flames, swirling sparks into the air. I hunched deeper into my cloak to ward off the chill of the night and another chill I couldn't explain.

Marta tucked the woolen blanket more snugly around my lap. "You won't lose anything by at least sending him a note of your arrival."

"What if I am a bother to him?"

"If you don't try to see him, won't you always wonder if he would have visited you?"

"Perhaps." I'd been honest with Marta about the nature of my relationship with Torvald, that he'd spent our wedding night on the floor and hadn't returned to my chamber since. She of all people knew of my growing feelings for him. I could hide nothing from her.

"I sense that he is falling for you, my lady," she said softly. "Don't give up yet."

I wasn't ready to give up. Not when we'd just begun. I could only pray he felt likewise.

Chapter 15

TORVALD

As the messenger finished delivering his news of King Canute and his advance with the Dark Warriors, my blood ran cold.

King Ansgar bolted up, tipping over his chair on the dais in his place of honor in the great hall of Likness Castle in Romsdal. In the next instant, Queen Lis was standing beside the king. Pale and thin from her illness, she still radiated beauty and strength as she took hold of the king's hand.

He clasped hers, as though she were the source of his life.

Was she? What would happen to him if we couldn't find the chalice to save her? And even if we found the chalice, we had no guarantee that it would renew her lifeblood and prevent her from dying.

I dreaded the weak man King Ansgar might become if Queen Lis died. I feared him dying inside like my father, and such a fear only prodded me with more urgency to find the chalice. Since my return last eve, I'd joined everyone in plotting strategy and discussing our options for taking the forest back from the jotunn. Gunnar and Sven had shared the details they'd learned in my absence.

And later, Gunnar had also informed me about his rapid wedding to Mikaela. Even now, at the head table, he could hardly take his eyes off his new bride, sneaking kisses throughout our noon meal. He seemed happier than I'd ever seen him before. His wedded bliss served to remind me of the fact that I, too, was a married man, and that I'd been content over the past two weeks with Karina and now felt empty without her.

"Dark Warriors?" King Ansgar pinned a hard look upon the messenger, who was dusty and grimy from his mission to deliver the news to the king as rapidly as possible. "I thought the Dark Warriors had been obliterated long ago."

The legends surrounding the Dark Warriors were frightening. Such men from the far northern reaches of Swaine lived in darkness for much of the year. As a result, they were rumored to be able to see as well at night as in full daylight. Thus, they were adept at attacking and decimating their enemies in the black of night.

Maxim, who had been sitting beside the king, conferred with Princess Elinor. Then he rose. "Your Majesty, if the Dark Warriors are indeed accompanying King Canute, then we are in grave peril."

From my spot at the side table with the other Knights of Brethren, I was fast coming to the same conclusion, especially for my home. Wahlburg would be one of the first places the Dark Warriors might attack. I'd told Karina and her family to leave by the week's end. But what if the enemy arrived in the dead of night before she had the chance to escape?

With a growl of frustration, I pushed to my feet, my heart pounding so hard that I could hear little else.

Across from me, Espen met my gaze. His expression was serious, and I knew he was thinking the same that I was—my bride was in danger.

I had to leave. Anon. I would ride all the way back to Wahlburg if I must.

Without asking permission for a dismissal, I stalked away from the table and toward a side door. I could feel the stares of everyone in the room following me, including the king.

"His wife." Espen spoke hastily. "Torvald is concerned for the well-being of his wife, since Wahlburg is near the border."

I was already out the door and didn't hear what the king or anyone else had to say about my departure. But as I hastened to leave the building, Espen's heavy footsteps echoed in the passageway behind me.

"'Twould be faster to send a messenger with a missive on ahead," he called.

He was right. Even so, I had to go. A clawing had started inside and was ripping me to shreds. I wouldn't be able to concentrate on anything else until I knew Karina was away from the danger.

As I exited the keep and started down the steps, Espen caught up to me. "You're going anyway?"

"Yes."

"Then I'll accompany you."

"I cannot ask it."

"You're not. I'm telling you."

"I am riding without stopping."

"Good," he said with an easy smile. "I am too."

We were saddled, mounted, and on our way within

the hour. I knew I was being disloyal to the king and his mission to find the chalice, but Gunnar and Sven seemed to have the details of the attack of the jotunn and Hardanger Forest well planned already. They didn't need my advice. And if possible, I would return in time to accompany them when we executed our mission.

Several of our squires rode with us, and we galloped the way we'd just ridden only a day ago. The clawing inside only worsened, making me grit my teeth so that I didn't shout out my frustration.

I didn't like or understand the strength of my reaction to this predicament. I told myself I was feeling this way because Karina was kind and sweet and innocent, and that as her husband, it was my responsibility to ensure her safety.

But something deeper jabbed me and wouldn't let me rest, something I didn't want to think about. And the question nagged me: how was it that I'd once believed I could ride away from my wife and never look back? During the journey toward Romsdal, thoughts of her had occupied nearly every waking moment. I'd relived our time together. And I'd relived our parting kiss more than anything else.

The images and thoughts and desires for her had woven throughout the fibers of my being, so that with each passing day I was more consumed with her. In fact, I'd even begun to contemplate doing what Gunnar was— including his wife as much as possible in his missions for the king. I'd learned that the king supported Gunnar's marriage and had given approval for the Knights of Brethren who were married to keep their wives with them, declaring that together they could accomplish more.

Was it possible that I could keep Karina with me? Two weeks ago, I would have scoffed at the notion. But now, after getting to know her, I ached for her and couldn't deny I longed for her presence.

We'd only just made it past the outskirts of Romsdal and arrived at a fork in the road when I spotted a party riding toward the city from the east. It was a fairly large group, with a dozen or so riders, and near the forefront was a large man with a wide girth, his red hair burning like a beacon in the midday sunshine.

Lord Royse? My pulse skipped in anticipation.

In the next second, I was frantically scanning the other faces. As my gaze landed upon the lone rider at the rear wearing a plain brown cloak with a braid hanging over her shoulder, I released a tense breath. Karina.

Karina

Wearily I brought my horse to a halt, grateful for the reprieve. I was saddle-sore from the long hours of traveling. But with Romsdal on the horizon, I'd encouraged myself to stay the course.

With a group of knights bearing down upon us, I guided my horse off the path to make room for them to pass by.

"Lord Wahlburg!" my father shouted.

I scanned the men, locating Torvald's broad shoulders, sturdy body, and strong bearing, and my chest seized with the keen need to see him again.

With each passing league we'd drawn closer to

Romsdal, I'd prayed I would have the chance to visit Torvald one last time. But I'd tried to keep my expectations realistic, especially when so many other responsibilities clamored for his attention, responsibilities much more important than me.

Would I have the chance now to speak with him? Or would he pass us by, since he clearly seemed in a hurry?

As Torvald reached our group, he reined in abruptly, hopped down, and strode past my father and the others without a word or glance, even though my father was rambling on about our travels and the danger.

Torvald headed toward me, his eyes affixed upon me and no one else. His jaw was chiseled with determination, and his hand on the hilt of his sword as if he would slice down anyone who stood in his way.

With each step closer he came, my heartbeat pounded harder with a strange anticipation. And when he halted beside my horse and looked up at me, his gray-blue eyes took me in from my head to my toes. "You are unharmed?"

"Yes, my lord. Tired but well."

He glanced on the road behind us, taking in every detail. "Is anyone pursuing you?"

"No," my father answered before I could. "We received the warning about the Swainian king and his Dark Warriors and left anon."

"Good." Torvald shifted his attention back to me and extended his hand.

Did he want me to dismount? I wasn't sure my legs would hold me if I stood, but I placed my hand in his and allowed him to assist me down.

As my feet touched the ground, my knees buckled. "I am sorry, my lord—"

Before I could finish my apology, he scooped me up and held me in both arms as easily as if I were but a babe. "I just got the news regarding King Canute," he said. "I was riding back for you."

For me specifically or for everyone? Inwardly, I chased the thought away. It didn't matter. He was here and concerned, which was more than he needed to be. "That is very kind. I would not expect it of you, not when you are so busy."

Around us, the others were using the break to dismount and stretch. Even so, I could tell we were the center of attention—or at least, Torvald was drawing looks. Were people wondering why he was bothering himself with me? I ought to insist that he put me down. I would be strong enough in a moment.

But he was studying my face with such concentration, I couldn't make myself say what I needed to. "I shouldn't have left you behind." His voice turned into a ragged whisper.

"Do not be harsh with yourself." I smoothed my hand over his scruffy cheek. "None of us could have predicted King Canute calling upon the Dark Warriors."

He leaned into my touch as if he relished it. Had he been worried about me? As usual, I couldn't keep my words from spilling out. "Regardless of the circumstances, I am happy that our travels have brought me to you again. I own freely that I was missing you and longing to see you here. Father wasn't sure if you'd have the time to visit with us before we boarded a ship—"

His lips fell upon mine with a hard, crushing kiss, one that weakened me and sent strange energy through me at the same time. I sensed his kiss was his way of telling me he was missing me and longing to see me too.

His kiss was short, and he broke away before I could gather my wits to wind my arms around him and press back. He was already striding toward his mount, carrying me as though he had no intention of releasing me.

I had no desire for him to release me, was too overwhelmed by the imprint his mouth had left upon mine to think of anything else.

When Torvald lifted me into his saddle, Espen coughed and spoke something like "more kissing" into his hand while smothering a smile. Torvald shot his friend a glare. "I shall have my wife ride with me because she is weary from the journey."

Espen coughed again and murmured, "Likely excuse."

Torvald's shoulders remained rigid as he held Espen's gaze.

The teasing didn't bother me. Instead, it made my stomach do crazy flips, especially at the prospect of Torvald bending in and kissing me again. Whatever his reason for placing me on his horse and having me ride with him, I wouldn't protest.

As he hoisted his hulking frame behind me, I was aware of every inch of him. Since I was riding side saddle, I was practically sitting on his lap. And as he took the reins, he stretched his arms out on both sides of me, boxing me in against his chest.

"Are you comfortable, my lady?" His voice was a

low rumble against my ear that sent tingles down my arms and legs. I had the urge to simply sit and let him whisper in my ear the rest of the day, but I could sense the attention yet upon us, and I knew I had to maintain the decorum expected of a lady.

I nodded, then I leaned into his ear. "I can think of nowhere else I would rather be, my lord."

His arms tightened about me. As he nudged his horse around and started toward Romsdal, I let my body melt against his, suddenly filled with so complete a satisfaction that it brought tears to my eyes. I'd never felt so cherished and wanted before in my life. Was it possible Torvald could learn to accept and love me after all?

Although he didn't kiss me again during the ride back, I could feel his breath near my temple and at my cheek. From the possessive way he held me, I sensed that he wanted to kiss me but was restraining himself around so many onlookers.

I spoke to Torvald of my doings before leaving Wahlburg Castle and then also relayed the details of our journey across the Moors of Many Lakes. He didn't say much in return, but the rigidness of his posture began to relax the longer I shared, and I hoped that was a sign he didn't mind my talking.

When we arrived at Likness Castle, situated protectively on a fjord with the city its footstool, I breathed in the familiar sea air. After growing up in Finnmark, a port city, I loved the scent of brine and fish, the cool, damp breeze, and the rhythmic crashing waves.

A dark woodland lay to the north of the castle. Thick trees and shrubs spread out as far as the eye could see. From the little I'd gleaned of the king's mission, the chalice was believed to be buried somewhere deep within. But apparently the forest was fraught with danger and rumored to have a jotunn living there.

Upon riding into the courtyard bustling with servants, I sat up straighter. "Will I meet the king and queen?"

"Yes. I shall introduce you to them."

I'd never seen royalty, much less entered into their presence, and I wasn't sure I could do so as graciously as would be expected of Torvald's new wife, Lady Wahlburg.

"Perhaps 'twould be for the best if I went with Father to an inn. Everyone is so busy, and I do not wish to—"

Torvald shifted his hand from where it was resting lightly upon his thigh and moved it to my hip. As his fingers settled there, words escaped me. All I could think about was the strong pressure and the warmth of his touch.

"What do you not wish?" His whisper brushed my ear, sending a delectable shiver down my spine.

"I do not wish . . ." What had I been saying? I couldn't recall a single thought from a moment ago.

"My lady?" His voice had a rare note of mirth.

"I do not wish to be apart from you." The whispered words rushed out before I could stop them. "No, what I mean is that I do not wish to disturb you any further, my lord. I have imposed enough today as it is. And I ought to change my garments into something cleaner, more suitable. Truly, I think it is best if—"

"Karina." His tone held a gentleness that halted my rambling. "You are beautiful already."

Saints and angels. Had he just told me I was beautiful?

"And the truth is," he whispered nigh my ear, "I do not wish to be apart from you either."

My entire body turned to liquid.

"You will stay here at Likness Castle. With me."

I wasn't sure if my heart could take any more heat.

"If you are agreeable," he added quickly.

I placed my hand over his still resting on my hip. "I shall always be agreeable to being with you, my lord."

He swept aside my braid, grazing his fingers along my neck in the same motion.

I gasped.

In the next instant, his lips pressed softly right below my ear.

I sucked in a sharp breath and was dizzy with a swirl of desire. What did his attention mean? Was this his way of showing me he was ready to give me his heart after all?

The touch of his lips was so brief that he was slipping off the mount before I could figure out a way to respond. He lifted me down and placed me on my feet reverently, as if I were worth more to him than anything else in the world.

I couldn't contain my joy. My smile bloomed quickly. Though the circumstances for our marriage might not have started as ideal, I held hope that eventually we'd be able to forge a strong and beautiful union.

Chapter 16

TORVALD

"YOUR MAJESTIES." I BOWED BEFORE KING ANSGAR AND QUEEN Lis. "I present to you my wife, Lady Karina."

Karina curtsied.

I couldn't take my eyes from her, hadn't been able to since seeing her upon her horse. Though dusty from her travels, she radiated the freshness of a spring bloom, even though she was clearly tired.

Now, as she straightened, I was tempted to sweep her off her feet, carry her to my chamber, and deposit her in my bed so that she could sleep. But first, I wanted the king and all my fellow knights to see my bride. She was not only the most beautiful maiden present, but she was the sweetest and kindest as well.

Karina's hand trembled in the crook of my arm. I squeezed her fingers to reassure her that she was perfect. She slid me a look, one filled with gratefulness.

I didn't deserve this woman. She was too good for me. But my heart overflowed with affection for her anyway, an affection that kept growing, so that now, at this moment, I could think of naught but her.

From the corner of my eye, I could see Espen grinning smugly as though he was the one who'd matched me with Karina. Lord Royse stood on the other side of Karina and was, for once, speechless. The wide-eyed awe upon his countenance in the presence of the king and queen almost made me smile. Hopefully, he would get what he sought—the respect and recognition of those among the nobility.

"We are glad you made it safely away from Wahlburg," the queen said to Karina.

Karina curtsied again. "Thank you, Your Majesty. While I am verily glad to be reunited with my husband, I will continue to pray for all those we had to leave behind, including Lord Wahlburg, who was too weak to travel with us."

At the mention of my father, I stiffened. In all my worrying, I had not considered his well-being. Even now, I couldn't summon any pity for him, not when he'd brought his own demise upon himself.

The king was glancing between Karina and myself, his eyes taking on a sparkle, one I hadn't seen there in weeks, maybe months, since before Lis grew sick. "Lady Karina, I can see that you are exactly the kind of woman Torvald needs."

"Thank you, Your Majesty." Her cheeks flushed, making her adorable freckles stand out all the more.

"It was clear from the moment he stormed out of here earlier that he is quite taken with you."

Karina quirked one of her delicate brows at me.

I kept my expression stoic. I had no intention of explaining anything. She didn't need to know how frantic I'd felt when I'd learned she was in danger.

King Ansgar's lips twitched up into a grin. "I never thought I'd behold the day when any woman could capture Torvald's heart. But 'twould appear you have accomplished it."

Capture my heart? The words rumbled through me, sending a wave of anxiety in their wake. I'd vowed I wouldn't give away my heart. And now, somehow, I'd not only given it to her but allowed her to take it captive.

"I am pleased for you both," the king continued. "And I wish you many happy years together."

Would our years together be happy?

I bowed my head before anyone saw the panic building inside me.

I somehow went through the motion of introducing Lord Royse and his son. And then I gained permission to assist them to their chambers. Though King Ansgar was polite, I could see his attention sliding back to Queen Lis— the concern in his eyes, the frustration creasing his forehead, and the tight pinch of his lips.

Right now, the king was consumed with finding a cure for his wife. Nothing else could compare to the importance of that. But was it time to cease the search for the sacred chalice when Norvegia was being threatened, possibly invaded, by King Canute's army and the Dark Warriors?

The Ansgar I'd once fought alongside and admired would have seen the greater peril and set aside his own desires and ambitions to do what was in the best interest of the nation.

Even if he wasn't willing to relinquish this mission altogether, maybe he should consider leaving a contingent while he led the rest of the army toward the border to defend the country against the invaders.

"You are frustrated with the king," Karina said as I escorted her down a passageway. Her servant Marta trailed behind us a short distance.

"He has my allegiance." I'd assumed I'd been able to keep a tight rein on my emotions, allowing no one a glimpse of my true feelings. How had Karina been able to see past my façade?

"He clearly admires and respects you."

"And I, him."

Karina's father and the others in their party were staying in a different wing of the castle. Had I been too hasty in bringing Karina to my chambers?

Now that I was leading her there, I couldn't send her away. The only thing I could do was keep myself busy with other tasks, at least until I could regain some of the control I seemed to lose whenever I was around her.

I'd seen what the loss of control had done to my father. He'd been so in love with his wife that he'd given her everything—his heart, body, and soul—and he'd been left with nothing. I didn't want to do likewise and end up empty like him. But was I already heading in the same direction, even though I was trying not to?

As we reached my chamber door, I swung it wide but then stood back. Karina moved past me into the room and Marta followed her. For just a second, I wanted to send Marta away and pull Karina into my arms and kiss her to my heart's content. But I fought against the urge and instead stepped further into the hallway.

"My lady, please rest." I bowed my head. "The servants will summon you for supper."

With that, I spun on my heels and stalked away, not daring to look back.

The Knights of Brethren had convened again with

Sven, this time in the antechamber. As I entered, the conversation came to a halt. The room was smaller than our meeting room at the royal castle, and it reeked of mildew and stale rushes. But it was private, and we could all fit around the table.

Gunnar stood and slapped me on the back. "Methinks someone else deserves the title of *Slayer*."

His comment brought a round of guffaws from the others. 'Twas the nickname we'd bestowed upon Gunnar for how easily he slayed the hearts of women everywhere he went.

I didn't give them the satisfaction of a reaction and instead sat calmly and quietly in my spot. I nodded at Sven, who'd paused his explanation as I walked in.

Immaculately groomed in the finest of garments with neatly trimmed hair and beard, the lord of Likness Castle carried himself with dignity and confidence, regardless of the red scars on his face that he'd received early in his life from a fire.

Though the disfigurement was prominent, Sven was already earning a reputation as a kind and generous lord throughout Romsdal. I'd only spoken with him a few times since my arrival, but on each occasion, I'd been impressed by his intelligence, bravery, and the goodness of his spirit. 'Twas obvious he'd allowed his challenges to shape him into a strong and worthy man.

The map of Hardanger Forest that Sven had sketched was spread out at the center of the table along with a diagram of the caves where the jotunn lived and where Sven had made his home.

Although Sven had done a sufficient job recreating everything he knew about the forest and the caves, the maps couldn't capture everything, and Sven had warned us repeatedly that the passageways within the caves were especially confusing. He was convinced the chalice was being stored in the heart of the caves, a deep cavern where the jotunn went from time to time.

Sven had only tried once to follow the jotunn down the dark hole, but the sulphureous scent as well as other noxious fumes had rendered him ill so that he'd had to climb back up. As a result of his failure, we'd discussed at length how to avoid being overcome by the fumes. Sven had suggested the possibility of a mask, but even then, no one knew how far down the hole went or how long the passage would take.

Of course, before we could descend, we had to eliminate the jotunn. Sven was convinced the jotunn couldn't be slain like a mortal man. He'd tried to kill the jotunn on several occasions during his early years as the jotunn's slave, but nothing he'd tried had succeeded.

Our goal was to trap the jotunn and then toss a net of heavy canvas over him, preventing him from looking at anyone. According to both Sven and Gunnar, the jotunn could place a curse upon a person by linking gazes with them, and the curse, once spoken, could not be broken.

I'd always relegated trolls to tales and myths, had never believed they were real. And I suspected the curses were nothing more than superstition.

Whatever the case, the jotunn was a deranged madman who had held the forest hostage long enough. From everything I'd heard about the snares, footholds, and pits that were hidden all throughout the woodland, they were cleverly designed by someone with a twisted and evil mind. Eliminating the jotunn would aid Gunnar and Mikaela's efforts to change the lives of the people of Romsdal—including the villeins—by giving them the forest for fuel and game.

Gunnar drummed his fingers on the table as he studied the diagram of the caves. He claimed that the wound he'd sustained during his last trip into the forest was healing, but the bandages around his calf were proof that the danger was all too real. "We have seen evidence that others are attempting to cut a path through the forest, which means Rasmus may still have men in the area."

"Do we know why Rasmus seeks the chalice?" I asked.

Kristoffer's eyes took on a sharp gleam. "I think we all know the answer to that. He intends to use the chalice to bargain with the king for the queen's life."

"We can't let him get it," Espen said through a mouthful of sweetmeats he'd scooped out of the bowl at the center of the table. "Mayhap we need to head into the forest sooner than we planned."

I agreed. We had to find the chalice before Rasmus could. Then we wouldn't have to worry about the king being put into a difficult dilemma of saving his wife or the country.

King Ansgar's expression was somber. "How much longer will you need to finish cutting a path?" He addressed his question to Gunnar.

"Three days?" Gunnar answered. "Maybe two, if we stay in longer."

Gunnar was leading the group in forging a path. Sven had tried to go back in to assist but had fallen ill every time he stepped foot into the forest. Gunnar hadn't wanted the older man to go in anyway and had insisted Sven was already doing enough to come to our aid.

"They have reached about here." Sven pointed to a spot on the map. "The closer they get to the caves, the more chances they have of drawing the attention of the jotunn." Apparently, the jotunn was most active at night, and they were at less risk going in during full daylight. Even then, they only worked at clearing the path for several hours at a time.

The king nodded. I waited for him to say three days was too long, that it would put our country at risk as we focused on finding the chalice instead of preparing for war. But he remained silent.

He'd already indicated that once the path was cleared, he wanted to be the first to go in wielding the Sword of the Magi against the jotunn. But everyone had agreed such a move was too risky, that the king needed to stay out of the forest and away from the jotunn's curses. The country needed him and his leadership, especially with the impending war.

As we once again began to plot where we could best trap the jotunn and how to go about it, the unease within me only swelled.

I wasn't sure how this race to find the chalice would end, but I didn't have a good feeling about it.

Chapter 17

Karina

Had I done something to offend Torvald?

All throughout supper, I waited for him to lean closer, to brush against me, perhaps even to hold my hand. But he remained stiff and uncommunicative. Surely I hadn't imagined his desire for me earlier when he'd ridden out to us?

I wore the same gown that I had to our wedding, the only fancy one Marta had packed. With all the gold embroidery, it was my favorite. I'd hoped it would please Torvald, but so far, nothing had.

I was all the more grateful for Mikaela and Gunnar, who sat with us and were easy to talk to, regaling us with tales of their encounter with the jotunn.

They'd shared with me the possibility that the chalice had some kind of healing power, and that the king was seeking it to cure the queen of her bleeding disease. Though most people still didn't know about the potential of the chalice, word was spreading, especially now that the king was in Romsdal.

"The curse," I said, twisting around my goblet and swishing the liquid inside. "I don't understand how the jotunn has the power to make curses."

Gunnar had his arm around Mikaela, cuddling her close. With brown hair and eyes, she was beautiful though unpretentious, as if she didn't realize exactly how exquisite she was.

Gunnar, however, seemed entirely aware of her beauty and couldn't get enough of her. He was constantly sneaking kisses, and his hands were always on her, rubbing her arm, drawing circles on her shoulder, grazing her neck, skimming her cheek.

At times, I flushed just watching them. And I felt a tiny pang of what I could only describe as jealousy. It was an unfamiliar feeling, one I would later need to repent of during my prayer time. The truth was, I wanted Torvald to hold and caress me the same way Gunnar did with Mikaela. But I had to remind myself that not all men were as openly affectionate. Some were more reserved, like Torvald. And I couldn't put expectations upon him that weren't meant to be.

Gunnar nodded toward the head table. "Maxim and Princess Elinor have been searching for more information about curses." The wiseman and woman were in a deep conversation with Sven, their gazes intense, their food forgotten. "From what they've learned from Holy Scriptures, 'twould appear that curses can be passed on for many generations. Some believe they go through seven generations before ending."

Torvald pushed away his trencher, finished with his meal. He wiped his hands clean, then rested them on his thighs.

He might not be openly affectionate, but that didn't mean *I* couldn't be, at least to some small degree, especially as I continued to try to win his heart. Though I was still naïve, I hadn't forgotten Marta's advice from before my wedding.

I placed my hand over his and gently squeezed.

He didn't move, not even to blink.

I left my hand where it was. "Is it always a bleeding curse?"

Mikaela gave a slight shrug. "Maxim and Princess Elinor have not discovered other curses, but that doesn't mean they don't exist."

I boldly brushed my thumb across the back of Torvald's hand. He still didn't react, but at least he wasn't pulling away. I wanted to regain the affection he'd shown me earlier, but I sensed I must break past more barriers he'd erected. "Then the queen's bleeding curse was given to her family by a jotunn?"

"No one knows for sure. But 'tis possible."

"I thought women were immune to the jotunn's curses." I traced one of Torvald's fingers, gliding along the length down to his blunt fingernail. Then I started on the next finger.

"Immune, no." Mikaela rested her head against Gunnar's shoulder, and he bent and kissed her temple. "But women are much safer than a man, since the jotunn is easily distracted by a woman's charm and beauty. The fables speak of women defeating trolls, but never a man."

Gunnar looked pointedly at my red hair. "Maxim said jotunns like red, which could account for the blood-red bleeding curses."

I finished tracing Torvald's last finger, and he didn't

budge. He'd told me during our last time together in the chapel that my touch weakened him. If that was true, then what was I doing wrong?

I started to lift my hand away, but in the next instant Torvald captured my hand within his, twining our fingers as though he had no intention of ever letting go.

When I peeked at him, his jaw twitched. A moment later, his gaze connected with mine. The heat within the depths of his eyes was so powerful it singed me and sent sparks all along my nerves.

In the middle of saying something more, Mikaela paused, glancing between Torvald and me.

Gunnar's brows rose, and his charming grin made an appearance. "Yes, indeed, my good man. You are smitten."

Torvald tossed a glare at Gunnar as though to stop him from saying anything more.

Gunnar chuckled.

I could feel Torvald begin to distance himself again, so I asked, "How will you find the chalice once you have reached the jotunn's caves?" I needed to distract Gunnar from teasing Torvald, and conversation about finding the chalice always seemed to do that.

Sure enough, Gunnar began to explain the dark caves where the jotunn lived, how Sven had helped him map them out since they faced the real peril of getting lost within the many caverns, which all looked alike and twisted and turned in an endless pattern of tunnels.

While Gunnar talked, I placed my free hand over Torvald's hand that was laced with mine. This time, I caressed the sinews on the back of his hand, making tiny trails and relishing the solidness of each finger.

As I finished with his thumb, he pushed back and stood so suddenly that I nearly gasped. He didn't release my hand, and instead tugged me to my feet along with him.

Gunnar halted mid-sentence. The other conversations around us tapered to silence, and the attention turned upon Torvald.

Again, his jaw twitched. "Please excuse me. I must speak with my wife in private."

My heart sank. Was he upset about my forwardness? Would he bid me to cease my touching? I had been rather brazen.

Gunnar and the other knights exchanged grins. Torvald's brows came together, and the sternness of his gaze seemed to warn his fellow knights against saying anything.

Gunnar spoke anyway. "Certainly. You go *speak* with your wife. *Speak* with her as long as you need."

Torvald guided me away from the table toward a side entrance. As we stepped into a dark passageway and left the great hall behind, I wanted to free myself and run back. I was afraid of what Torvald might say. Nevertheless, I breathed deeply and forced myself to remain calm.

He pulled me along for several paces, then he halted abruptly. The sconces gave off little light, but it was enough to witness the determination in his face.

I had to apologize before he said something. "My lord, I was too forward. I beg your forgiveness—"

He released a low growl, then bent down and took possession of my mouth. Each stroke was hungry, almost as if he hadn't eaten in days and I was his feast.

And each move was hard, the weight of his body flattening me against the wall.

The kiss was consuming. *He* was consuming. And there was no place else I wanted to be except with him.

"Torvald?" I broke the passionate connection.

His lips chased mine.

I turned my head, which only gave him access to my neck. As he began to make a trail of kisses down to my collar bone, I clutched him, my breathing only escalating. "Torvald?" I had to tell him how I felt now. It was burning within me and couldn't be contained.

"Hmm?" His voice was low and did funny things to my insides.

I lifted a hand to his face and guided him back just a little, allowing me to see his half-lidded expression. I traced the scar on his cheek. "Where did you get this scar?"

"My first battle against the Ice Men." He murmured the words before resuming his kisses.

"I fear losing you." The words weren't what I'd planned to say. But they were true.

As if the seriousness of my statement penetrated his passion, he paused. He pulled back enough to look into my eyes, his nose brushing mine.

"You need not fear it."

"But with the jotunn and now the war?"

"I am a seasoned warrior."

"What about when I am a nuisance, when you finally tire of me? I also fear what will happen then." I was being too open as usual. But the words spilled out, nonetheless.

"Does a man ever tire of breathing air?" His

whisper was gruff and scraped me raw.

"No, but—"

"You are the air to my lungs." His eyes were dark and brooding and serious. "You bring me life."

This connection with him, it was beyond anything I'd ever known or experienced. And it was dizzying and delightful all at once. I lifted my face up to him, wanting him to know I would kiss him again if he wished for it.

He bridged the distance and captured my mouth again, as intense and passionate and purposeful as always. I would go on kissing him here in the hallway all night if he was agreeable.

At the clearing of a throat behind us, Torvald broke our kiss. Even without his lips against mine, I was drowning in him, couldn't think, couldn't move, couldn't speak.

He glanced toward the newcomer but didn't back away from me. His arms rested against the wall on either side of my body, and now he leaned his head against the wall too, his ragged breathing stirring the hair near my ear.

"Sorry to interrupt." It was Espen. "But the king is convening a meeting with the Brethren."

"Right now?" Torvald's question rumbled with irritation.

"Yes, the queen just nearly fainted and is being taken to bed. As soon as the king finishes accompanying her, he expects us to meet him in the solar adjacent to their chambers."

Torvald tensed and seemed to be reining in his tongue. Finally, he gave Espen a curt nod. "I shall be there soon."

After we were alone again, Torvald remained where he was, pinning me to the wall.

I didn't want to move, loved being with him, loved the brush of his breath on my skin, loved the slight pressure of his chest against mine. The truth was . . . I loved him. Yes, I'd fallen in love with my husband quickly, almost instantly. But how could a woman not love a man like Torvald?

As much as I longed to linger with him, I didn't want to be the cause of him being late for a meeting with the king. "You must go, my lord." My whisper was shaky and unconvincing.

He hesitated but a moment before pushing away from the wall and from me. He rubbed the back of his neck, blew out a tense breath, then held out his hand. "I shall walk you to our chamber."

"But the meeting with the king—"

"He can wait." Torvald's voice took a stubborn note, one I suspected had to do with the frustration with the king I'd noticed earlier.

I accepted his hand, and he laced his fingers through mine.

He didn't seem to be in a hurry to reach our chamber, and as usual, was quiet while I spoke of my admiration for all his friends and the people I'd met. When we reached the door, I still felt flushed and full from his kisses, but I smiled up at him, hoping to put him at ease.

His gaze dropped to my mouth, and his eyes darkened.

My stomach tightened with need—the need to fling myself in his arms and kiss him again. But I couldn't. Not now. "When you are finished with your meeting, shall we take a walk in the gardens? I should like to spend more time with you before I have to leave for Finnmark."

He hesitated.

"If you are too tired—"

"No."

"Then I shall wait for you."

His hand tightened within mine. "See that you do."

I extricated myself and opened the door. As I stepped through, his gaze followed me with a yearning that made me tremble.

"I believe myself to be in love with you, my lord." The words tumbled out in a whisper.

He froze.

Rapidly I closed the door and leaned back against it, mortified and amazed all at once that I'd spoken the words. I suspected my declaration would frighten him. He was a puzzle of hot and cold, and I never knew what to expect from him. And this was one time I was better off not knowing.

Chapter
18

Karina

I sidled near the door of the king's chamber. I was attired in my plain cloak and ready for a walk in the garden with Torvald. Was the meeting at an end?

I'd paced the length of my chamber for at least an hour, awaiting Torvald's return. With each passing minute, my worry had mounted. I'd feared that my pronouncement of love had scared him and that he would avoid me the rest of the night.

Finally, Marta had advised me to seek him out. If he was still in his meeting, then I would know he wasn't purposefully staying away. And if the meeting had adjourned, then I'd need to track him down and find a way to smooth over my rash words.

I paused and listened through the door.

Voices rumbled from within.

I let the tension ease from my shoulders. They were still meeting, which meant he hadn't been evading me. Even so, there was still the chance he might not want to see me again tonight. And before he could escape, I needed to try to win him once more until eventually I won him over fully.

I was getting closer, wasn't I? Surely all the signs were there, signs that he cared about me.

Silencing my inner worries, I pressed my ear against the door. I didn't want to eavesdrop. I merely wanted to discover how much longer I needed to wait. But at the sound of Torvald's voice, raised in irritation, every thought of returning to my chamber fled.

"We cannot wait," he was saying. "We must instead send out the word to the chieftains and nobility alike to amass in Vordinberg with all haste."

"Two more days," the king replied. "Maybe three. You heard Gunnar tell us that's all the time they need before we're able to go in and look for the chalice."

After hearing Gunnar's tales about encountering the hidden traps for himself, I was glad they were taking every precaution to make the way safe before commencing the attack. Regardless, the more I knew about the plans, the less I wanted Torvald to go into Hardanger Forest.

"Even if we had a week," Torvald spoke again, "could we really put so many of our best men at risk? Why not choose a few select knights to finish the mission, and send the rest to the front?"

Silence fell over the room.

I pushed away from the door. Did they suspect I was listening? What if someone opened it and caught me there?

I was in the wrong for eavesdropping on the conversation and needed to go. I started to back away, but the king's next statement halted me. "Now that you are married, Torvald, I thought you would understand better how I feel."

"Understand what?"

"Understand what it is like to love a woman beyond anything else, so much that you are willing to move heaven and earth to find a way to keep her."

"You are wrong, Your Majesty." Torvald spoke with a distinct note of disdain that pricked me. "What I understand is that you have let a woman turn you into a weak man."

"A weak man?" The king's tone took on an edge of offense.

"Yes. Instead of using your head and doing what is in the best interest of the nation, you are letting your heart rule and doing what is best for you and your wife."

Torvald's comment caused a chorus of raised voices.

"'Tis not weak to love," the king called. "I've witnessed the affection you have for your wife. If our situations were reversed, surely you would do the same thing."

Torvald didn't immediately respond.

I tensed as I waited for his answer, not sure I wanted to hear it.

When he answered, his tone was low. "I have seen that loving a woman can destroy a man from the inside out. I will never let that happen to me."

Was Torvald referring to his father? Lord Wahlburg had confided in me the devastation he'd felt upon his wife's leaving. As a lad of eight, Torvald had lost not only his mother but his father too. And perhaps that's why he'd vowed not to give me his heart, because he'd watched his father give away everything and have nothing left.

A heaviness settled over me at the magnitude of Torvald's loss and heartache. Now I understood the push and pull between us, why one moment he seemed as though he wanted to be with me and the next, he wanted to be far away.

Could I convince Torvald that he didn't have to hold back any longer? That I wouldn't leave him?

"Loving a woman doesn't have to destroy you." This came from Gunnar.

"It will not destroy me because I will never allow myself to love." His announcement sliced like a blade, twisting painfully, cutting off my air. It wasn't a surprise, not after he'd already made clear from the start of our relationship that he didn't intend to give me his heart. At least he'd been honest.

The problem was that I'd allowed my optimism to cloud the situation. I'd believed if I worked hard enough, I could win him over, could eventually make him love me.

Maybe I was winning his affection to a small degree—if his kisses were any indication. But he'd already determined never to love a woman wholly and completely for fear doing so would make him a weak man like his father. If he found himself unable to resist my overtures, he would only end up loathing himself, and I didn't want that to happen either.

I had to acknowledge the truth—loving him was hopeless and would only end in disaster.

Soundlessly, I began to back up. The pain in my chest prodded me to get away. I made it out of the passageway and to the nearest stairwell. As I descended, my feet carried me swiftly. The pressure in my chest and the sting in my eyes signaled tears, but I blinked them back, not willing to mourn over this situation.

Instead, I hastened to a side entrance of the keep. Then I fled into the garden, where I could be alone to think without Marta or anyone else offering me advice. As well-meaning as my maidservant had been, I'd pushed Torvald into something he wasn't ready for—might never be ready for. I should have taken the little he had to give me and been content with that. Then maybe I wouldn't have fallen in love with him.

As I lowered myself to a stone bench in the darkness, I wrapped my cloak closer. Yes, the problem was that I was desperately in love with him. I loved him more than I'd ever believed I could love any man. And because I loved him, I wanted him to be happy and content.

At the burning in my chest, I bent over and buried my face in my hands, letting silent tears wet my cheeks.

I would leave for Finnmark and never bother him again. That's what I'd do. It's what he wanted, and now I knew why. So that we could remain married in name but live two separate lives.

Such an arrangement would give him the resources he needed to care for the people of Wahlburg, but he'd also have his freedom. Without me and our attraction constantly tempting him, he wouldn't have to worry about becoming a weak man like his father. He could remain strong and secure and continue doing his duty for the king.

Yes, he needed me to leave as soon as possible. The longer I stayed, the harder this was getting for him, and I didn't want that.

As I sat up, the elegant coil that Marta had worked so hard to style came tumbling down. I twisted the braid. In the moonlight, the red glistened brightly.

The red.

My fingers froze. I stared at my hair, letting an idea formulate.

Before leaving, I could do one more thing for Torvald, for everyone.

Chapter 19

TORVALD

THE MEETING WITH THE KING HAD BECOME TOO PERSONAL, AND I was more than ready for it to be over. But to my frustration, it seemed to be dragging on.

I'd long past put aside my yearning to take a walk in the garden with Karina. In fact, I had no intention of seeing her at all the rest of the night, maybe even the rest of her time at Likness Castle. I would send her and her kin on their way to Finnmark via the first ship leaving on the morrow.

Until then, I would find another room to sleep in. And if not, I would lay out a pallet in the great hall with the lesser knights.

If this meeting ever ended . . .

King Ansgar paced back and forth the length of the room. Gunnar and I stood together on one side of his chamber, and Espen and Kristoffer stood on the other. The other six Knights of Brethren were also standing, but since they were newer to the group, handpicked by Ansgar after he became king, they didn't offer as much advice. Or perhaps they didn't feel the freedom to be as forthright as the four of us. After all, we'd been Ansgar's closest companions before he'd become king. We'd spoken unreservedly to him then, and he had asked us to continue.

In fact, in our meeting room back at the royal residence in Vordinberg, King Ansgar had brought a round table in to replace the rectangular one that had been there. He'd said he wanted one without sides or heads so that we could converse as equals, no one of us more important than another. That was why the Knights of Brethren no longer had a Grand Marshal.

The king valued our opinions, but now that he'd allowed his love of his wife to cloud his judgment, he was being stubborn.

I tugged at the top of my doublet, the layers of clothing having grown warm in the crowded confines of the chamber.

Gunnar clamped a friendly hand upon my shoulder. "Methinks I have to be the one to tell you the truth."

"The truth about what?"

"The truth is that you're already in love with your wife."

"No—"

"It's as clear as daylight."

I shook my head, but the rest of the Brethren and the king were already echoing their agreement.

Panic churned deep within. "She is a kind and compassionate woman, and she wins over everyone she meets."

"She has indeed won you." Espen grinned smugly. "I could see it the first time I watched you interact with her at Wahlburg. 'Tis obvious you love her more than anyone or anything."

Kristoffer's lips quirked into one of his dignified smiles. "You could not leave the great hall fast enough this eve to get her alone and kiss her." The rest of the men guffawed while I shook my head, trying to deny it. But they were right. Each caress of her fingers against my hand had stoked the fire within me until I'd felt like I would burn up if I didn't kiss her.

"Her outer beauty alone would be enough to sway a man," Kristoffer continued, "but 'tis clear she is even more beautiful inside."

Kristoffer was usually right about most things, and in this case, I couldn't argue with him. "Maybe I have grown to care about her—"

"You are consumed with her and would die for her." Espen's eyes dared me to contradict him.

The churning turned into an acid that worked its way through my stomach and up into my throat. Espen was right too. I was consumed with Karina. She occupied my every waking and sleeping thought. And I'd been ready to ride back to Wahlburg earlier today to make sure she was safe, and would have sacrificed my life for her if necessary.

I lowered myself to the closest bench against the wall, bent over, and pressed my face into my hands. A groan pushed for release, but I held it inside. What had I done? I'd vowed never to fall in love with a woman, never to give away my heart, never to let myself become smitten. And in a fortnight, I'd thrown my life away. I'd done the very thing I'd warned myself against: I'd turned into my father.

"I have become a weakling." My words were strangled.

"Listen, my good man." Gunnar sat down beside me. "Selfless love for a woman doesn't turn a man into a weakling. Instead, when we push ourselves hard to give, sacrifice, be patient, and love unconditionally, we actually become stronger."

Then why hadn't my father become stronger? Hadn't his love been giving, sacrificing, patient, and unconditional? The question pushed for an answer, but I swallowed it. I'd told Gunnar only a few generalities about my father being sick, but I'd never gathered the courage to be honest with my companions about the true extent of his condition.

"Mikaela makes me into a better man. With her by my side, I can do greater things than I could on my own. And I'm sure Ansgar feels the same way about Lis."

The king was a humble man and never put on airs around us. But I wasn't able to revert to using his first name and dropping his title the way Gunnar could.

King Ansgar released a tense sigh. "I agree with you both."

I lifted my head, his weary tone moreso than his words grabbing hold of me.

"Lis does make me stronger. She has many qualities I lack. But I'm also letting my selfless love turn into a selfish obsession."

Love turning into an obsession? Was that what had happened to my father? Maybe he'd had a selfless love at the beginning of his marriage, but when he'd been faced with the prospect of losing his wife, he'd turned inward, thought only of his own needs and the emptiness of his life.

"I want to put her happiness above my own." King Ansgar's voice dropped. "But lately, I've been thinking of how devastated I'll be without her, and I'm elevating my own happiness above hers and even above the people I serve."

My father had put his happiness—or lack thereof—above everything else including me. As a result, he'd wasted years of his life. If only he'd recognized it earlier, would the knowledge have made a difference?

Could such knowledge make a difference with me and my love for Karina? I didn't know if I believed myself in love with her yet as my friends had declared. But whatever I felt was intense. I'd always felt things more forcefully than most people, just like my father. Could I allow myself the possibility of loving her selflessly without it turning into selfish obsession? Or was I simply doomed to repeat his mistake?

King Ansgar resumed his pacing, but this time his steps were firmer and with more purpose. "Gunnar, how many men do you realistically need to capture the jotunn?"

"According to the current plan, we will need a large force to surround him, toss the canvas, and then bind him."

The king kneaded the back of his neck. "And what if he curses any of the knights before you're able to cover his head?"

Gunnar's gaze slid to me, and the seriousness of his expression told me that the nature of the mission into Hardanger Forest would be difficult no matter the number of men who went in. His eyes held mine, asking me a silent question: Would I risk everything, including my life, and go into the forest with him? Without the rest of the Brethren or the king's army to assist us?

I nodded. I didn't need him to ask. This was our mission, and I planned to see it completed no matter what happened.

Gunnar stood and faced the king. "We need two

men—Torvald and me."

All eyes swung to us.

"Just two?" The king's brow rose.

"Yes. While a large force might help push the jotunn back into one of his caves, two men will not draw as much attention to themselves."

I tensed, waiting for King Ansgar to insist that two wasn't enough, that he needed to send in more to accomplish the task.

He stared straight ahead, a war raging across his countenance. How many lives would he put at risk for Queen Lis? Not only sending men to their deaths in Hardanger Forest but also in neglecting the border and allowing King Canute to storm into Norvegia unhindered?

As if hearing the unspoken direction of my thoughts, the king lowered his head.

"We will find the chalice, Your Majesty." I pushed up from the bench. "I vow we will not leave the forest without it."

'Twas possible Gunnar and I wouldn't make it out of the forest alive, that in spite of the strategizing, mapping, and removing of the traps, we still wouldn't be able to outsmart the jotunn. Even so, the two of us had to be enough. Everyone else was needed to defend the country against Swaine's invasion.

"Very well." King Ansgar's voice held resignation. "Torvald and Gunnar shall stay behind with Lis. The rest of us will depart on the morrow and prepare for war."

Even as I bowed my head in acknowledgement of Ansgar's command, grateful for his humility and willingness to see reason, a strange sense of unease settled inside me, especially as I thought about Karina and the possibility that I might die in the forest and never have the chance to be with her.

Gunnar bowed his head too, but as sadness etched the corners of his eyes, I guessed he was realizing the same—that once he went back into the forest, he might never see his bride again either.

"I would go in after the chalice myself, if you would let me." King Ansgar glanced between the two of us.

"No, Your Majesty."

"No." Gunnar spoke at the same time that I did.

"But the sword—"

"Norvegia needs you," I said. "Without you, who will stand in King Canute's way of taking the throne? Especially if Rasmus is directing him."

The king pressed his lips together as if he wanted to argue. After a moment of silence, he spoke, this time his voice laden with emotion. "I'm grateful for your willingness to do this for me, for Lis. If our roles were different, I hope you know I'd do likewise for you."

"Of course you would." Gunnar offered a smile, but it lacked its usual carefree air.

I said nothing. But I knew the truth of the king's words. He was a good man and had proven again he was the right man to be king by showing true humility and courage. We had minced no words this eve, but the honest discussion—while difficult—had challenged us to be better men.

He started toward the inner door that would lead to his private chamber. Of course, if this was to be his last night in Romsdal, he would want to spend the rest of it with Lis.

While Gunnar and I weren't leaving immediately into the forest, I could see him inching away. Was he thinking, like the king, that his time with his wife was limited and that he wanted to make the most of whatever he might have left?

In all my years of going to war, I'd never feared injury or death. I'd always been willing to give up my life for my country. But now at the prospect of dying in a few days' time, my gut tightened. Perhaps I'd never had a reason to live. Never a reason to come home. Never a reason like Karina.

After everything the Brethren had spoken about what true selfless love looked like, I wasn't sure yet if I was ready to send her away, not until I had the chance to find out if I was capable of that kind of love. Could I give her my whole heart without losing myself in the process?

Did I dare keep our arrangement to take a walk in the garden?

With a shake of my head, I forced thoughts of Karina away. 'Twas selfish of me altogether to consider fostering any feelings toward her when I might be dead by next week. If I made it out of the forest alive, then maybe I would give myself permission to explore more of what could be. But until then, I would do best not to let anything permanent develop between us.

Chapter 20

Karina

I hadn't realized exiting Likness Castle would be so easy. With the additional servants and laborers coming and going from the castle to help serve the king and queen, I'd left the gardens and walked away unnoticed among the others, especially because my long brown cloak had covered the rich glowing gold embroidered into my gown.

Now, it was even easier to enter Hardanger Forest without anyone stopping me. The new cleared path was marked with a flag, and even with only a candle, I could see the way well enough.

Several dozen paces into the woodland, I paused, turned, and held up the flickering flame. I'd expected a watchman on the castle wall to notice my light and send someone to investigate. But no alarms had been sounded, which meant no one was paying the forest any heed. And why would they? After all, they wouldn't expect anyone to be foolish enough to enter the forest in the dark of night without weapon or warrior.

Maybe I should have told someone of my plans, even if only Marta. Of course, while awaiting Torvald's return to his chamber, we'd talked about the jotunn, and I'd told her that I'd distract the jotunn with my red hair if Torvald would allow me to accompany him. But Marta and I concluded that he'd never agree to it.

Torvald. My heart ached each time I reviewed the words he'd uttered in the king's chamber earlier: *I will never allow myself to love.*

Although 'twas possible for some people to change and grow, Torvald's statement had been edged with finality. He'd proven he was a determined man so far, and I had no doubt he would remain determined to keep himself from love, no matter how much he might enjoy kissing me now and then.

I glanced around, my gaze landing upon a skeleton hanging in a high branch overhead. "Devils and demons."

With a shudder, I lowered my candle so that all I could view was the path directly in front of me. I'd heard the tales of the many people who'd gone into Hardanger Forest over the years. Some had been hungry and starving villeins needing game. Others were men sent in by the lord for one reason or another.

Whatever the case, I'd learned that no one had ever faced the jotunn and made it out of Hardanger Forest alive until Gunnar and Mikaela had gone in along with Mikaela's friend Frans. Even then, both men had been injured, and Frans had nearly died.

The gallant men who'd accompanied Gunnar in cutting the path had lived. But they hadn't ventured in far enough to be in constant danger from the jotunn.

Over the next few days as they continued to cut the path, their peril would only increase.

As it was, I'd reach the end of their trail soon enough and would have to make my own way to the jotunn so that I could bargain with him. Mikaela had spoken of the jotunn being willing to accept meaningful exchanges, had given him an important shell for Sven's freedom.

I'd pondered what I could present the jotunn and had decided to offer him my friendship in payment for the chalice. Hopefully with my red hair, he'd be even more enamored with me than he'd been with Mikaela and would do my bidding.

Perhaps I was naïve to believe I could win him over with kindness rather than force. Perhaps I was naïve to believe I could walk in and not face any danger or injury. And perhaps I was naïve to think I could avoid a curse.

But I'd also resolved to face whatever came. If Torvald and the other knights were willing to sacrifice so much, why shouldn't I do likewise? Truly, any harm I brought upon myself would be worthwhile if I could keep Torvald safe.

I could only pray he wouldn't discover I was gone. When I didn't return to my chamber, Marta would have no reason to worry and would assume I'd been successful in seeking Torvald out. When Torvald came back to the chamber to slumber—if he came back— he'd likely conclude I'd gone to the chapel to pray. If by morn someone finally noticed my absence, I would be close to returning, if not already out of the forest. At least, I prayed it would be so.

I started on my way again, picking up my pace,

wanting to make good time since the hour was already late. From everything I'd heard, the journey to the heart of the forest would take several hours, if not more. Thankfully, the path was wide enough that I didn't have to worry about my skirt and cloak getting tangled in the branches and brush. The air was damp and dank. And like on all Norvegian nights, the temperature was quickly falling.

I shivered, not sure whether it was from the cold or from fear of the unknown.

"Pray, Karina. Pray." Though I wasn't in the chapel, I began to recite the words of the prayers I'd learned during my time in the convent. The simple trusting prayers soothed my soul and reminded me again that I was doing this for the man I loved.

No, Torvald didn't love me in return. He'd rejected me and was casting me aside, so much like my father had done. But just as I'd resolved to love my father anyway, in spite of his tendency to overlook me, I would love Torvald too. Loving others was necessary and good when they were easy to love. But loving others was even more necessary when they were challenging and difficult and didn't reciprocate.

I walked and prayed for what seemed like hours, until I finally found myself at the end of the cleared path. Although the overgrown trail ahead was difficult to see, I forged onward, stepping carefully, Gunnar's tales of buried traps foremost in my mind.

What would the traps look like? How would I know where one was located?

As I stepped on a twig, a snap punctured the silence. I jumped quickly backward, my pulse speeding. My mind filled with the story of Gunnar hanging upside down, his leg caught in a snare.

Maybe I was better off drawing the jotunn to me rather than continuing to venture forward.

"Hello?" I called.

I listened for a response, but not a cricket, bat, or even an owl made a sound, almost as if I were completely alone. Perhaps I was. Perhaps the jotunn had scared away every living creature.

I took several tentative steps, then halted. "Hello, jotunn. I would like to speak with you, if you will be so gracious as to allow it."

Again, eerie stillness filled the darkness.

"Please!" This time I shouted, unaccustomed to raising my voice after living for so long constrained by the rules of silence in the convent.

The echo of my cry was all that I heard.

Lifting my shoulders, I forced myself to keep going. In the next instant, my foot slipped, the grass and leaves beneath me gave way, and a black cavern opened up in the ground. Though I fought to jump back, I was too late. I found myself sliding down, dirt and windfall tumbling with me.

A moment later, I landed against the hard earth with enough force to knock the wind from my lungs. The light from my candle had extinguished. In fact, at some point during the slide, I'd lost my candle altogether.

Spluttering, I pushed myself up, wiping my face free of what felt like spiderwebs, trying to draw in a lungful of breathable air. As I stood, the dirt walls closed around me on all sides, constricting and tight.

I skimmed the walls, and more dirt crumbled away, cascading over me. I hoped my fingers would connect with tree roots that I could use to hoist myself upward. Maybe there were rocks available for footholds. But I could feel naught but damp earth.

I was trapped with no way out.

Panic slithered around me, cold and cruel like a serpent circling and drawing tighter. All my life, I'd never had to worry about anything. I'd always been safe and well taken care of. I'd had everything I ever needed and more. And now, I was in a place where I was absolutely helpless with no way out.

The darkness was so black I couldn't see my hand in front of my face . . . except for the strange glow near my feet. Maybe my candle hadn't gone out after all.

I glanced down only to find there was no flame. Instead, the embroidered golden threads around the hem of my gown radiated a soft light.

A whisper of gratefulness dispelled the dark thoughts that had been crowding in. In the midst of my black moment, Providence had provided a way to comfort me, to bring me light, and to assure me that he was always with me.

I shed my cloak so that the golden threads on the rest of my gown could shine in the darkness. During my tumble, several of the golden threads in the skirt had come loose, likely having snagged on twigs. But now with the dress uncovered, the hole was no longer dark, and I breathed in the assurance that I would be fine throughout the rest of the night as I awaited morn and the appearance of Gunnar and the laborers who would arrive to work on the trail.

"You are pretty, lady."

A voice overhead startled me awake, and I glanced up to find a large man peering down at me, framed by a burning torchlight. His features were oddly over-sized, especially his nose, which protruded unnaturally from his face. A patch of coarse white hair stood straight up from the top of his head. Other than the tuft, his head was devoid of hair, giving his round face an almost childlike quality.

This must be the jotunn. Who else could it be?

I quickly stood and brushed the dirt from my skirt. "My name is Karina. I'm pleased to meet you."

"Karina. That's a pretty name." His voice also had a childish quality.

"Thank you. Are you the jotunn?"

"Yes." He didn't seem dangerous.

"I was hoping to visit with you." I wrapped my cloak around me.

"You were?"

"I will need you to find a way to hoist me up first."

"I can do that, lady." He scrambled backward and disappeared for several moments. When he returned, he thrust a long branch into the hole.

When my fingers clasped around it, he tugged me up as easily as if I weighed naught more than a feather. As I scrambled over the edge, he steadied me with a gentleness that took me by surprise. After the tales I'd heard, I hadn't been prepared for the jotunn's tender treatment.

Upon straightening, I realized he was taller and bigger than any other man I'd seen, towering over me by several feet. He wore scraps of ragged clothing and boots open at the toes showing curled toenails. Everything about him was unkempt and dirty, as though he hadn't groomed or taken a bath in a long time—if ever. Whether he was a mythical troll or simply a misfit who'd been cast from society and relegated to living in the forest, I would treat him with the kindness everyone deserved.

He held his torch above me and stood back to take me in. One eye was half-closed, and the other was blinking. "Your hair is red, lady."

After it had come loose from the fancy coil in the garden, I'd purposefully left it one long plait. "Do you like red hair?"

His lips cracked into a wide grin revealing missing teeth and the gray stubs of any that remained. "Yes, it is very pretty."

I took a deep breath and plunged forward with what I knew I must do. "I was hoping you might be willing to make an exchange for the chalice."

His smile faded, and his eyes narrowed.

"'Tis not for me that I make such a request," I added hastily. "I implore you on behalf of the king and queen of Norvegia. The queen is dying, and the king would like the chalice to bring healing to the woman he loves."

The jotunn's wide forehead began to crease, and he started to shake his head.

I had to make him see reason. "The king is noble and good and is willing to sacrifice everything for his wife. What would you do for a woman you loved?"

He stilled, then earnestness filled his eyes. "I will love you."

From the simplicity of his statement, this giant man was more childlike than I'd realized. What kind of response could I give him that would be both kind and truthful as well as understandable? After all, I hadn't come to hurt him. "That is very sweet of you. Your offer is kind. But I am newly wed to a man I already love very much."

The jotunn's countenance darkened at once, and I could feel his goodwill slipping readily away. Without it, he would curse me, kill me, or both.

"I cannot offer you my love," I said as gently as I could. "But I can offer my friendship."

"Friendship?" The blackness of his anger fell away, replaced by curiosity.

This jotunn was volatile—switching from one emotion to the next in less than a heartbeat. I needed to tread carefully. "Yes, I offer you my honest and true friendship in exchange for the chalice." I held out my hand.

His gaze dropped to my outstretched hand as though he didn't know what to make of it.

I extended my hand further. "Shall we shake to seal our bargain?"

Slowly he reached out his hand and placed it in mine. His was twice the size. His fingers were short and his nails bitten down to almost nothing. The grooves of his skin were darkened with soil.

Even so, I clasped his hand in mine and gave a firm shake. "See, we are friends."

"Friends." A smile lit up his face.

"And now, as my friend, I hope you will be willing

to help me find the chalice so that I might help save the queen's life."

He stared at my hand within his.

I waited. Would he deny me again?

He shook my hand a second time. "Friend, I will take you to the chalice."

"You are so very kind." I smiled in return. "Thank you."

With a nod, he released me. Then without another word, he turned and began to make his way through the brush in the direction he'd come. I didn't know if he was guiding me through the danger or taking me toward the worst yet. Either way, I'd started down this path, and I couldn't turn back now.

But there was one thing I could do. I quickly tied the loose golden thread in my hem onto a branch. I gave a gentle tug, and it began to unravel. Later, when I needed to make my way out of the forest, I would have the glowing golden thread to guide me.

Chapter 21

TORVALD

I PACED IN THE PASSAGEWAY OUTSIDE THE GREAT HALL. THE HOUR was late, and most of the knights and other staff were already stretched out and asleep on pallets near the main hearth. Though I'd planned to bed down with them, a part of me resisted—the part that wanted to spend my remaining days with Karina.

I had no right to go to her. I'd likely hurt her by my avoidance over the past hours, especially when I'd failed to show up for our garden walk.

Even though I hadn't spent the time with her, I'd thought of her and little else. And I'd thought of all that Gunnar and King Ansgar had spoken about love. Was it possible I could learn to love my wife the way they did theirs? They'd proven they could treasure their women without the adoration becoming an obsession.

But could I?

Maybe I needed to try. Maybe I'd given up before allowing myself the chance to prove I could do it too.

"What are you doing here?" In a long tunic and with

bare feet, Espen shuffled toward me from the opposite end of the hallway that led to our guest chambers.

I paused in my pacing but didn't answer his question, too embarrassed for him to know my predicament.

Stifling a yawn, he stopped several feet away and rubbed a hand across his eyes. "You're making matters more complicated than they need to be, Torvald."

"And what do you know of my matters?"

"I know you're avoiding Karina and have been ever since you married her."

Had it been that obvious? "'Tis not your concern."

"I also know you want to love her freely, but that you're too afraid to allow yourself the possibility."

How could Espen see so clearly what I was just beginning to understand? "Why are you here? Go back to bed."

"I'm hungry and am raiding the kitchen."

I waved him past me. "Do not let me stop you."

He grinned. "Oh, you won't. Don't worry."

I watched him warily, waiting for him to nag me again.

He stared back.

"What?"

His grin slipped away. "Stop squandering the love she's offered you. Cherish every moment you have with her, for you don't know how many more moments you have left."

He was right. I was wasting the short amount of time that remained. And the truth was, I had no guarantee of any beyond what this week held. I could make use of the last few days with her, couldn't I?

With a curt nod, I started past him.

"You're welcome," he called after me.

As I headed down the hallway, my body was suddenly

keyed with anticipation. My feet picked up their pace as if they had a will of their own. I bounded up the stairs, taking them two at a time.

By the time I reached the door to my chamber, my breathing was labored. I paused in the dimly lit hallway, drew air into my lungs, and tried to calm my suddenly racing heart.

If she was asleep, I wouldn't disturb her. But if she was awake, I'd apologize for my absence earlier and ask her if she wanted to take the walk.

As I opened the door, my gaze went first to the bed. It was empty. The covers hadn't even been turned down.

"My lady." Marta rose from a chair. "You're back—"

I stepped further into the room. Karina wasn't anywhere to be seen. And if her maidservant was awaiting her return, then she was out somewhere.

My pulse slowed to a sickening crawl. What would a lone woman be doing at this time of the night?

"Where is she?" My question came out harsh, and my body was tense.

Marta took a step backward and bumped into her chair. "I thought she was with you, my lord."

"Clearly, she is not." I couldn't allow myself to think the worst of Karina.

Marta grasped the chair as though it could defend her from my wrath. "Earlier, she was worried you might not want to spend time with her. So, I encouraged her to seek you out. She went to where you were meeting with the king, hoping to find you there."

If she'd lingered outside the king's chamber, what if she'd overheard the conversation? I hadn't exactly been positive about my marriage or my desire for her.

"My lord," Marta said, "I thought you must have been

done with the meeting and gone on a walk together. But if she isn't with you, then I don't know where she is."

I cast aside my suspicions. There was only one place Karina would be, especially if she was hurt by something she'd overheard.

I spun on my heels and exited. I practically ran back the way I'd come until I reached the chapel in a separate passageway off the great hall. I pushed open the door but stopped short at the emptiness of the small room. Though a sconce flickered with low flames, I didn't need its light to realize Karina wasn't there.

With my heart pounding louder, I raced to the gardens. I checked the stables, thinking perhaps she'd found a new litter of puppies or kittens. But I saw no sign of her anywhere.

"Where did she say she was going?" I demanded as I returned to my chamber, disheveled and hot and breathing hard.

Espen paused behind me. With a wedge of cheese in one hand and a leg of lamb in the other, it was clear he'd succeeded in raiding the kitchen. "Karina is gone?"

I didn't know whether to go beating on each door in the castle until I found her or trust that she was remaining faithful to me and our marriage. Surely she was, even if I'd been cold and kept her at a distance.

I pushed down the swirling storm within. "If not the gardens, chapel, or stables, where else would she be?"

Marta shook her head, rising again from her chair. "If not with you, she would have returned. I know my lady, and she is careful to live above reproach."

"Is she staying with her sister-in-law?"

"No, her father came earlier to give me instructions about the ship leaving on the morrow. He was looking for her as well."

"Then where is she?" This time my question came out an angry shout.

Marta dropped into the chair and cowered.

I felt Espen's hand against my bicep, to restrain me if necessary.

"What is happening?" Kristoffer appeared in the door in his tunic and braies.

In the next instant, Gunnar was shoving past him, quickly donning his clothing. "What's amiss?"

"Torvald's wife is missing." Espen's pronouncement was grave.

I began pacing back and forth with hard slapping footsteps, not caring that I was working myself into a frenzy. I needed to find out where Karina was and go after her.

"Do you think someone abducted her?" Kristoffer's question was as practical and astute as always. "With her vast fortune and now her connection to Torvald, it's possible someone may demand a payment."

The very thought of anyone touching Karina turned me nearly rabid. I had to stop and draw in a breath before I took out my wrath on one of my friends.

"You are her maidservant," Kristoffer persisted. "Did she make mention of any place she might think of going?"

Marta was frozen in her chair, her eyes wide upon me, as if I were a vicious animal who would attack her at the slightest movement.

I took another breath and then attempted to speak as calmly as possible. "Tell us all you know, Marta." My request came out a desperate plea.

Thankfully, it seemed to loosen Marta's tongue. "Before leaving to seek you out, my lord, she mentioned how she would like to go with you into the forest and aid with seeking out the jotunn."

At her words, it was as if someone clamped a fist around my heart and squeezed the life from it.

"She said her red hair could help win over the jotunn," Marta continued. "That maybe she could gain the chalice by asking rather than taking, so that none of you men would have to get hurt."

I bent over at the waist, unable to breathe. Karina had gone into Hardanger Forest. No doubt about it. It was exactly the thing she would do. Her compassion and kindness knew no bounds, and if she could help, she would see it as her God-given duty to try.

I had to go after her.

"If we leave now, we may yet be able to catch up with her," Gunnar spoke solemnly.

I swallowed the bile at the back of my throat.

"I'll go too," Espen said.

"And I," Kristoffer added.

Gratefulness wound through me for these men and their support. They were better friends than I deserved. I straightened, but before I could answer, Gunnar was already shaking his head. "With the jotunn being more active at night, the risk is too great for all of us to go in. Just Torvald and I will go after her."

I stalked over to where my chain mail hung on a peg on the wall, not willing to waste another second.

"We will tarry at the forest's edge." Kristoffer glanced at Espen for confirmation.

Espen took a bite from the leg of lamb and nodded. "If you need us, then you must call."

At some point, my squires had arrived at my chamber, although I hadn't seen or heard their approach. Now one of them lifted the chain mail to assist me in donning it.

However, I wouldn't need anyone's assistance but my own. I was angry enough that I would tear the jotunn limb from limb. Then I would carry Karina out of the forest and never let her leave my side again.

Chapter 22

Karina

The jotunn finally stopped. We'd walked for so long I was afraid I would come to the end of my golden embroidery thread before reaching the destination.

I glanced down at my skirt. The glowing light was gone. All that was left was the intricate pattern around my waist and a few spots upon my bodice.

Would the remaining thread be enough for the journey through the caverns? In listening to the knights describe Sven's diagram, they'd indicated that the winding tunnels were complex.

I needed the golden thread now more than ever.

"Here we are." The jotunn held his torch up, illuminating the rocky hillside covered in dark brush and trees and large boulders. A gap between two tall stones at the base of the hill revealed the entrance.

The last part of the journey had become more difficult as the terrain turned rockier. I'd struggled to keep up with the jotunn, especially since I was doing my best to unravel the golden thread without causing it to break.

From the measured steps he took, I knew he was keeping to the strange path he'd developed, one that prevented him from falling into a snare. Sven had shared the pattern with Gunnar and the others cutting the path through the forest. But I couldn't make sense of it, especially in the dark, and was all the more relieved I would have the golden thread to guide me out.

I conversed with the jotunn the entire way so that he wouldn't suspect I was leaving behind a trail. He hadn't offered much information about himself, but he'd seemed to like the things I told him about myself, my childhood, my going to the convent, and then my recent marriage.

From time to time, his anger had flared—when he'd bumped his head or stumbled. Each time, I'd feared he would turn and curse me. So I'd worked all the harder to keep chattering, diverting his attention to other things each time.

"Do you stay warm enough here during the winter?" I asked, climbing down into what looked like a ravine with a brook running through it.

"Yes. My fire will keep us warm."

I paused. This wasn't the first time he'd spoken as though he intended for me to stay with him. Did he think I would remain through the night? Or did he have more sinister plans?

Although the jotunn had a childlike demeanor, the longer I was with him, the more wary I'd grown, especially as I'd witnessed the gruesome and torturous traps that we sidestepped. Did he have a black heart? Had I been naïve to think my kindness would be enough?

Whatever the case, I'd ventured this far into the forest, and I couldn't stop now.

I followed him through the ravine to the tall opening between the slats of rock. As I stepped inside after him, a waft of cold air greeted me.

"The tunnels are so interesting." I unraveled the golden thread as we moved deeper into the dark passageway. "How do you think the caves were formed?"

"Water pressure during a flood." The jotunn's answer was so quick and certain that I knew he believed it. But when had there been a flood in Norvegia? There hadn't been any mentioned in the historical legends that I'd heard about, except of course, the Great Flood ages ago.

"The rock formations are very pretty. I love the mixture of colors." The lines and layers of reds and browns swirled with darker veins of black. But as we turned first one way and then another, I realized the rocks all looked the same. How could anyone navigate without getting lost?

With growing urgency, I pulled at the golden thread. How much farther could I go before it ran out? I could only pray we would reach the place where he'd hidden the chalice soon.

The real question was, once he gave it to me, would he allow me to leave the caves? Or would he try to keep me here forever?

Torvald

Gunnar kept up a punishing speed, leading the way down the path he'd helped to carve.

I suspected he kept the pace for my sake, knowing I would have pushed past him if he'd slowed. As it was, the trek deep into the jotunn's domain had taken longer than I'd wanted, especially because we would have to slow down once we reached the end of the cleared path. At that point, we would have to go at a crawl in order to avoid the traps.

Just thinking about the traps and the possibility that Karina might even now be languishing in one turned my blood cold. What if she'd stepped into a snare and was hanging upside down from a high limb? Or what if she'd fallen into a pit of sharp spikes? If strong and savvy men like Gunnar and his bondservant hadn't been able to avoid such pitfalls, how could a sweet innocent woman like Karina? She could very well be injured or even dead by now.

The thought only prodded me. "Faster," I called to Gunnar as I pushed up behind him. "We need to go faster."

"Hold up." He stopped abruptly, and I slammed into him.

He threw out his arms to prevent me from going around him.

"What?" I growled.

The torchlight cast a glow over the wildly overgrown

forest ahead, telling me we'd reached the end of the path.

He stared at a dark spot but a dozen paces away. A hole. "The trap wasn't uncovered when we were last here."

Panic barreled into me. "Karina?" I shoved past Gunnar, heedless of the peril to myself. Upon reaching the hole, fell to my knees and held my torch above it, my muscles tensing.

It was empty.

I sat back on my heels and expelled a shaky breath. "Maybe she stepped near it but retreated in time to keep from falling in."

Gunnar crouched beside me and fingered the edge of the hole in a place where the earth had crumbled away. "It looks like someone slipped in here or perhaps crawled out."

"How would she get out?" I gauged the depth, and it was at least the length of two full-grown men. And it was straight up and down, with no incline and no footholds for climbing.

Gunnar skimmed his fingers along the ground, uncovering a candle—likely the one she'd used to light her way. He pushed aside the leaves and twigs. Underneath, in the damp earth, was the outline of a boot that was double the size of any I'd ever worn. "The jotunn was here."

I was good enough at tracking to realize the print was recent. Had Karina fallen into the trap only to have the jotunn come and pull her out? Was she already within that monster's grasp? I didn't have to think too long to know that's what had happened. The jotunn had her as his prisoner.

I prayed the jotunn was so enamored by her beauty

and red hair that he wouldn't hurt her. But just the thought that she might now be suffering made me sick to my stomach.

I stood abruptly. "We need to go. Now."

Before I could stride forward, Gunnar grabbed my arm and held me in place. "If we want to help her, we must traverse the rest of the distance with caution. Neither of us will do her any good if we're hanging upside down in a tree."

Impatiently, I waved him ahead to lead the way. He'd studied Sven's map and could avoid the traps much better than I. As he took a step beyond the hole, my gaze snagged on something glowing on the ground. It winked and then seemed to disappear. I took another step, then it came back into focus.

Gunnar noticed it too, because he bent and swept aside the overgrown brush.

"What is it?" I leaned in.

Carefully, he plucked at something. As he lifted it, my mind scrambled to make sense of what we were seeing. It appeared to be a fine piece of thread.

Golden thread.

My pulse sped with a mixture of relief and hope. "'Tis Karina's."

"From her gown?"

"Yes." She was extraordinarily stunning in the white dress with gold thread, always irresistible but more so when wearing it.

"It appears to be glowing."

"Because it is. 'Tis the special dye Lord Royse uses in his textiles."

"Fascinating." Gunnar fingered the thread. It was thin but sturdy. The light coming from it wasn't noticeable from a distance, but it would provide enough glow to guide us.

Gunnar began to trace the thread forward. "Perhaps she left it for us, so we would know which direction to go, to help us avoid the traps."

Knowing how selfless Karina was, I guessed she had departed in the night, hoping not to bother anyone. She probably hadn't anticipated us coming after her and had unraveled the thread so that she could find her own way out.

Whatever the case, we'd been given this miracle, and I prayed that the golden thread would lead us to her before it was too late.

Chapter
23

Karina

I released the last of the thread, letting it fall to the floor of the dark passageway.

I needed more. Frantically, I ran my fingers over my bodice, searching for a string I'd possibly neglected. But I'd already scanned my garments a dozen times and couldn't find any more of the glowing thread tucked away.

I had to figure out another means of marking my trail, or I would be hopelessly lost. Already, after following the jotunn through the caverns for what seemed like leagues, I had no idea where we were. I wouldn't be able to find my way back to the narrow opening without the thread, especially if I had to traverse the route in the dark.

Pausing, I jerked at the linen shift underneath my skirt. The rip echoed against the stone walls.

The jotunn halted. As he spun, he narrowed his eyes upon me.

So far, he hadn't noticed the thread I'd left in my

wake. I couldn't let him suspect anything now.

I gave him what I hoped was a friendly smile. "You must be very smart to find your way through all the tunnels without losing yourself. I am completely turned around and would never be able to locate the exit again, not without help."

As with the other times, my smile and my kindness seemed to distract him and defuse the situation. "I've lived here a long time."

"If I lived here a hundred years, I still do not think I would know it the way you do."

He shrugged, then plodded on with his torch, the tight quarters forcing him to go slow. Even hunched over, his large frame hardly fit through some of the narrow spaces.

Moving forward, I rapidly unraveled the linen and let it fall to the ground behind me.

As we reached the end of a particularly long descent, we ducked through a low opening, and I found myself crawling out into a cave—the largest that I'd seen yet.

The jotunn thrust his torch into a slot in the wall, illuminating the scant furnishings: a fire pit with a stack of cut wood nearby, a pallet with a few ragged blankets, a low three-legged stool, a dented and blackened pot, snowshoes hanging from the wall, and a stack of leather-bound books.

"This must be your home. It certainly is cozy." Or perhaps this was where Sven had lived.

"Cozy?" He gazed around the room as though he'd never taken stock of it before. In some ways, he was a child—a simpleton—in a giant body. And again, I couldn't keep from thinking that though he might believe himself to be the jotunn, a troll, he was naught more than a man-child who'd been abandoned in the forest long ago by a family who didn't want him.

The chalice wasn't anywhere in sight—not that I'd expected it to be. But a part of me had been hoping it would be visible, perhaps out on display.

"Is this your main living area, or do you have other rooms you live in too?"

He paused, as though he didn't quite know how to answer my questions. "This is your home now, lady. You stay here in this cave."

So, he did intend to keep me here, maybe make me his slave like he had Sven. "And where do you stay?" I tried to keep the waver out of my tone, but my fear was mounting.

He pointed toward a tunnel on the opposite end. "My cave is over there."

During the feast, the men had spoken of the chalice being in a deep hole that only the jotunn could descend. Was the hole in his chamber?

"Will you show me your home?" I circled the hearth toward the other tunnel.

The jotunn's brow furrowed. "No, lady cannot go beyond this room."

I stopped. I'd diffused his anger thus far. If I went into his home, I had the feeling he'd erupt in true fury.

Even so, I had to push him to bring me the chalice. It was why I'd come. "You told me you would give me the chalice in exchange for my friendship."

"A friend will stay here with me always." He waved a hand around the cave.

He wasn't accepting mere words of friendship. No, he was requiring something much more difficult. He wanted me to prove my friendship by remaining with him.

Could I really do it? Could I live in the middle of Hardanger Forest with the jotunn as my only companion for the rest of my life?

Surely no one would miss me, at least overmuch, and I wouldn't have to worry about being a burden to anyone. Torvald would be spared having me as his wife, and my father would be spared having me in his home.

The jotunn was watching me as though he could see inside my head. Did he have the ability to sense the truth about people? Did he know he could trust me even if I couldn't trust him?

I swallowed all my reservations. "Very well. I will stay here with you." I would make this sacrifice to keep Torvald safe. "But first I must give the queen the chalice."

"You can leave it at the forest's edge for her."

"That is a reasonable request. And I shall do it. You may even accompany me to see that the deed is done."

He studied me a moment longer. Then he smiled, a childlike innocence returning to his expression. "You're nice, lady. I like you."

That was good, wasn't it? Even if a future in the forest with the jotunn wasn't what I'd anticipated, maybe I'd find new purpose here. But even as I tried to convince myself that I would adjust to solitude and silence again, my heart thudded a hard beat of protest against my chest. After the love and passion I'd experienced with Torvald, the thought of never seeing him, never speaking with him, never sharing his touch sent a wave of despair through me. Could I really go through with leaving him forever?

My thoughts returned to the previous eve, to the way he'd kissed me outside the great hall with such ardor as though he truly cared about me. But just as quickly, my mind filled with his assertion echoing from the king's chamber that he would never allow himself to love me.

I squared my shoulders. What choice did I have when he didn't want me? I'd declared my love to him, and he'd spurned it.

The jotunn started toward the dark passageway that led to his chamber. "Wait here, lady, and I'll get the chalice for you."

Chapter 24

TORVALD

AS I SLID MY FINGERS ALONG THE GOLDEN THREAD, IT FELL AWAY. I grasped it, but it was no longer there.

My heart plunged into a darkness as black as the tunnels we'd been traversing.

"What's amiss?" Gunnar whispered from behind me.

"She ran out of thread here." I held out the torch we'd decided to bring. Even though the light would give us away to the jotunn if he glimpsed it, we'd decided it was safer to bring it with us than to have nothing.

Now I lifted it, hoping for some clue that might keep us moving in the right direction.

Gunnar unrolled the parchment containing Sven's drawing of the tunnels. He studied it, moving his finger along one path and then another. He paused somewhere in the middle. "I think we're here."

Thinking and *knowing* were two different things. We couldn't afford to speculate. Not with Karina's life at stake.

I took several more steps forward, scanning the stone

walls and the floor. I couldn't straighten, and after walking in the stooped position, my neck and back ached. Nevertheless, I pressed on, my need for Karina driving me relentlessly.

With her golden thread to guide us, we'd sped through the forest, going much faster than we would have otherwise. I could only pray we'd be able to find her in time to save her from the jotunn and his evil plans. I still didn't believe he had the capability of cursing people, but I'd seen the evidence of his demented mind all throughout the forest, and I couldn't get to Karina fast enough.

"Perhaps we should mark the trail with something," Gunnar whispered again, "so that we can find our way back to the golden thread."

He was right. We didn't know how much farther we would have to go before finding her.

I pulled out my sword. "Shall I carve a rut in the floor?" As I lowered the tip of the blade, I froze. There, ahead, was another thread. It didn't glow like the other one, but it lay on the ground, nonetheless.

"She has started another trail." I touched the thin linen almost reverently, amazed again at Karina's ingenuity. Not only was she determined and daring, but she was intelligent and inspiring. I didn't deserve a woman like her, but I wanted her more with every passing hour.

If I could save her from the jotunn and if we both made it out of the forest alive, I vowed to do better and try harder to be worthy of her.

"She has done well." Gunnar examined the thread now too. "Not many would have such ingenuity."

We were getting closer. I could sense it. And I could faintly smell the sulphur Sven had warned us about.

As I started forward again, I picked up my pace,

trailing the new thread. Within minutes, a glow of light broke the darkness ahead. I lifted my sword, my body tensing.

Sven claimed the jotunn couldn't be killed—at least, not the same way a mortal man could. But I intended to try. At the very least, I could disable him enough to grab Karina while Gunnar tossed the canvas over him. Even now, I could hear the rustle of Gunnar removing the canvas from the bag slung over his back.

As we crouched low through a narrow passageway, the light brightened. I motioned for Gunnar to remain silent and leave his torch behind. He nodded, having worked with me long enough to know what my signals meant.

I inched to the end of the tunnel, being careful not to make a sound. As I glanced out into a cavern the size of a bedchamber, my sights landed upon Karina. She stood at the opposite end of the cave and was peering down another dark tunnel. Her back was facing me, but I didn't spot any injuries.

I suspected the jotunn was somewhere on the other side of the dark passageway and that Karina was waiting for his return. How long had he been gone? Would I be able to usher her away before he came back?

Motioning to Gunnar to stay where he was, I straightened and started toward Karina. Since the floor was covered in ashes, my footsteps were soundless. As I drew closer, I could sense the tension in her shoulders, and she was fiddling with the loose hairs at the end of her braid.

When I was but a foot away, she spun then gasped. Her wide blue eyes connected with mine, rounding first with surprise and then with dismay.

She started to speak, but I lurched toward her and clamped a hand over her mouth. Then I snaked my other arm around her waist and dragged her into a hard embrace, my relief at finding her alive and unharmed overwhelming me.

I pressed my lips against her forehead almost savagely before moving my mouth to her ear. "Do not alert the jotunn to my presence."

She nodded, her eyes still wide.

"How long until he returns?" I asked, lifting my hand from her mouth.

"Any minute," she whispered.

"Then we must go now." I started to guide her toward the tunnel where Gunnar waited.

She shook her head and struggled to free herself.

I kept moving, determined to leave now.

"No," she whispered.

At the echo of the word against the stone walls, I halted and once again clamped my hand over her mouth. I glared at her and hoped she could read the steel within my expression and realize I wouldn't be swayed from taking her away, no matter what she said or did.

She raised her hand to my cheek, grazed the stubble, and then touched my lips.

Under any other circumstance, I would have relished her boldness. But in this moment, I could only think about how desperately I wanted to get her away.

"Chalice." The word was but a mumble beneath my hand, but it was distinct enough.

I released her mouth and angled my head so that she could speak directly into my ear.

"He is bringing me the chalice." Her whisper was soft this time. "Wait for me at the forest edge. I shall bring it to you there."

I found her ear and pressed my lips there. "I shall not leave this place without you."

She wound her arms around my neck and clung to me, as if she was just as desperate as I was. Then she whispered in my ear again. "The jotunn has agreed to let me give the queen the chalice."

I should have taken encouragement from her declaration, but instead it filled me with renewed dread. "What did you offer in exchange?"

She hesitated, then she shook her head. "You must go, Torvald. Before he returns and sees you."

"Never." The word in her ear echoed with the passion of all I was feeling, but I didn't care. "I shall never leave you."

Standing on her toes, she buried her face into my neck. "I did this for you, to keep you from being cursed. Now please go."

She'd come here for me? After the way I'd treated her, why would she take this kind of risk on my behalf?

I couldn't allow it. But arguing with her would be futile. And we were only wasting time. I released her, and then before she could stop me, I jogged across the chamber and entered the dark tunnel.

I could hear her footsteps chasing after me. Her fingers grasped my arm, and she tugged, attempting to pull me to a stop. But I pressed onward. The jotunn had clearly instructed her not to come down this way, and she was dutifully obeying him.

But I was not so compliant. I pushed onward into the blackness.

Chapter 25

Karina

I had to stop Torvald from going into the jotunn's forbidden chamber.

I wanted to shout, plead, and cry until he went away. But any noise would only draw the attention of the jotunn. Already the scuffling of our footsteps would likely summon him from wherever he'd gone.

And I couldn't let him look upon Torvald, or he would surely curse him and make him a slave just as he'd done to Sven.

I jerked at Torvald's arm again. But he didn't slow his steps.

Even though I'd been inexplicably relieved to see him in the cave just moments ago, I didn't want him here. I may have worked out an exchange with the jotunn, but Torvald wasn't the type of man who would do any bargaining. No, Torvald would plunge his sword in and fight to the death. But this time, I feared it would be his death and not the jotunn's.

As we came to the end of the passageway and

entered another cave, Torvald stumbled and would have fallen if not for my grip on his arm. As it was, he tottered at the edge of what appeared to be a deep, dark hole in the floor. Strange heat emanated up along with the strong scent of sulphur.

I swiftly dragged him back, and this time he didn't resist. In fact, he scrambled into the doorway, pulling me with him well away from the chasm.

The only light was what remained from the torch the jotunn had left for me in my cavern. It wasn't much, but thankfully it provided enough glow that we could take stock of the jotunn's home. The room was small, the size of a closet, with naught in it but the hole in the ground.

At the scuff of footsteps in the tunnel behind us, I turned to view Gunnar making his way toward us, his brow furrowed, a canvas tucked under his arm, and his knife unsheathed.

In answer to an unspoken question Gunnar seemed to be asking, Torvald stepped aside and nodded pointedly at the hole ahead.

Gunnar halted and eyed it, his gaze homing in on a loose slab of stone on the floor. He cocked his head back toward the other cave, indicating that he wanted to have a private word with Torvald. When they were a safe distance away, they commenced a whispered conversation so soft I couldn't make out what they were saying.

A moment later, Torvald returned to my side. He brushed against me, pressing his mouth to my ear. The contact, as before, sent a tremor through me. It didn't matter that we were in the middle of the jotunn's lair. I couldn't help the way my body reacted to his nearness.

"When the jotunn climbs up," Torvald whispered, "you need to take the chalice from him."

"He told me not to go in his cave. He will be angry and refuse to give me the chalice."

"Tell him you were afraid without him near."

"He will sense I am lying and be even angrier."

For a long moment, Torvald didn't respond. Instead, his breathing resounded in the hollow of my ear, making me think of how much I loved him. The prospect of danger befalling him sent me into despair, so much that I closed my eyes and leaned against him, needing his support.

His fingers wrapped around the leather tie at the end of my braid. He tugged it off and then began to unravel the strands.

Now was neither the time nor place for him to caress my hair. Not only were we in the midst of a crisis, but Gunnar was standing but two feet away, watching us.

Even so, I couldn't find the strength or will to stop Torvald. His fingers stumbled over themselves in his efforts, but soon enough my hair spilled over my shoulders and down my back. He wound his hand in, drew up a fistful of my hair, and pressed a kiss to it. Then before I knew what he was doing, he unsheathed his knife and severed a lock.

I was too surprised to speak.

Torvald pushed it into my hand. "Give this to the jotunn in exchange for the chalice. You need to do so before he climbs all the way up."

I took the lock. It wasn't much. As long and thick as my hair was, I wouldn't miss it. Even so, I'd already made a bargain with the jotunn, and I doubted he'd accept something as insignificant as my hair now.

Before I could protest, Torvald released me and moved into the jotunn's chamber. Gunnar was fast on his heels, both of them skirting the hole. Torvald flattened himself against the wall in one corner, and Gunnar hid himself in the other. From their positions, I guessed they intended to somehow jump out and attack the jotunn from behind when he climbed up, perhaps as soon as I made the exchange.

I didn't like it. In fact, I hated that they were here putting themselves at risk. And I hated that the jotunn would come to harm. Even if his soul was dark and depraved, I wanted to believe that no one was beyond the saving grace and love of God.

From deep inside the hole came a clanging echo. The jotunn was climbing up.

With trembling legs, I moved into position in front of the hole, then braced myself for when he would see me standing there. What else could I do now but brave the jotunn's wrath and pray that somehow we would all survive?

Chapter 26

My muscles tensed with each pound of the jotunn's boots against the rung of a metal ladder inside the hole Sven had told us about. After counting at least fifty rungs, I'd finally given up my tally. All I knew was that the hole was steep.

Where did it lead? To the very pit of Hades itself? Perhaps that would account for the heat and scent of sulphur.

As the sounds of the jotunn's ascent drew nearer, Karina stiffened and shrank back from where she was waiting.

The soft light from the other cave illuminated her. It turned her red hair into burnished copper and seemed to place a halo above her head. Though her face was shadowed, she radiated beauty as pure and innocent as a rare gemstone.

The plan from moments ago had seemed workable. Gunnar and I had both agreed to let her stay and exchange a lock of hair for the chalice. Once she had the chalice in her possession, we would toss the canvas over the jotunn's face, force him down the hole, then seal the opening with the stone lid that lay on the ground behind it. If the jotunn didn't give her the chalice, we would need to wrest it from him first.

But now with the jotunn's approach, the plan seemed foolhardy. So much could go wrong that would put Karina in danger. We should have forced her to leave.

Maybe even now I ought to tie her up and carry her away. How could I bear watching her come face to face with the jotunn, especially if he was angry at her for coming into this chamber?

The footsteps clanked louder. I didn't know how many more rungs he had left, but I suspected less than a dozen. That wasn't enough time to whisk her to safety. I would have to proceed with the plan, regardless of how badly I needed to protect her.

A large hand appeared at the mouth of the hole first, then a tuft of hair. Within the next instant, the jotunn's entire head emerged. Although I couldn't see his face, I guessed he hadn't yet noticed Karina standing there. Instead, he was mumbling under his breath and focused on hefting himself up.

As he lifted his other hand to the surface, he held what could be none other than the sacred chalice. It was a bright golden cup that rested on an elegant stem and was engraved with fine detail that I couldn't see clearly in the darkness.

He placed the chalice on the ground and pushed it away from the hole, likely to give himself two free hands to aid in the rest of his ascent.

I nearly lunged forward at the realization of what he'd done, giving us the perfect opportunity to seize the relic.

But with only the greatest self-restraint, I held myself back and willed Karina to grab it instead.

Thankfully, in the next instant, she swiped it up. But instead of retreating and running, she knelt in front of the jotunn as his shoulders and upper body rose out of the hole. I knew she was only trying to be fair and kind, but I groaned inwardly, nonetheless, even as I motioned for Gunnar to hasten and toss the canvas over his head.

At the sight of her kneeling there, the jotunn halted. "Lady, you disobeyed my order to stay out of my home." The jotunn's voice was loud and petulant with a childlike quality.

My muscles hardened. And I attempted to clear my mind as I always did before I went into battle. I operated ruthlessly when I was singly focused on my enemy. That's how I'd gained my reputation as one of the fiercest warriors in all of Norvegia.

My sword already unsheathed, I pushed away from the wall. It was time for action. I'd waited long enough.

Next to me, Gunnar was taking action too, moving the canvas as quietly as he could.

But even as I tried to keep my focus on the enemy and the task at hand, my gaze strayed to Karina, so beautiful and enticing with her long red hair falling all around her.

She was my wife. The woman I'd vowed to love and cherish and protect for as long as I lived. From now on, I'd never be able to go to war or engage in battle so singly focused. Instead, I'd always have her on my mind. I had a duty to her. And that duty was more important than anything else. Not because I was weak or obsessed. But because I'd made her a promise when we wed.

Suddenly I understood King Ansgar's desire to save the queen. He wasn't weak or obsessed either. He was doing his best to fulfill his vows. Vows that were more important than his own happiness and fulfillment.

"This is for you." She held out the lock of hair I'd severed as an offering to the jotunn.

He accepted it almost reverently.

"I hope you will take it in exchange for the chalice instead of my staying in the forest with you as your friend."

Staying in the forest as the jotunn's friend?

I didn't have time to process the bargain she'd made other than one thought: I'd never allow it.

The jotunn stroked the lock she'd given him, clearly distracted. It was time to act. Gunnar flapped the canvas and tossed it. And I lifted my blade and brought it down upon the jotunn's shoulder.

He roared out in pain as the heavy canvas fell over his head.

I raised my weapon again, needing to throw him off balance and force him down into the hole. But before I could do so, he snagged Karina's hand and twisted it, even though he was blinded by the canvas.

She cried out and struggled against him.

This time I thrust my sword into his back.

His agonized scream echoed off the stone walls.

I waited for him to weaken and let her go. But his grip didn't waver.

Gunnar was sliding the stone over the hole. But he wouldn't be able to put it into place, not until I found a way to force the jotunn to release her.

I fought back my mounting panic. I was failing. And that wasn't something I was used to.

I jabbed my knife into the tender spot underneath the arm that he was using to grasp her, and I twisted it as hard as I could, my desperation lending me strength.

He howled his anger.

As though sensing the jotunn weakening, Karina jerked free. As she did so, her momentum caused her to fall back away from the hole. With the chalice in hand, she scrambled, her eyes wide upon the jotunn, as though seeing his deadliness for the first time.

While I loved that Karina always chose to see the best in people rather than the negative, this was a case where she needed to realize that she couldn't help everyone. Whether the jotunn was a man or a demon, perhaps we'd never know. But what was clear was that the jotunn had chosen the way of evil, likely long ago, and he'd festered in it ever since until it had overtaken his heart.

Now all that mattered was that Karina was free and far enough away that he wouldn't be able to get ahold of her again.

"You betrayed me, lady," he cried from underneath the canvas, rage and pain filling his voice. He began to push the canvas off his head. "Now you must pay."

I couldn't let him get free, couldn't let him glimpse into her eyes just in case there was validity to the cursing.

"Go, Karina!" I shouted. "Get out now!"

But Karina was breathing hard and seemed frozen in place. And the jotunn was scrambling out from the canvas quickly. He'd be free in just a few seconds.

I couldn't let the creature bring any harm to Karina. Had to stop him.

The canvas fell away, and I lunged again, this time aiming for his head. But as I swung my sword, he ducked, avoiding the blow. In the same move, he thrust a blade at me. It was the longest knife I'd ever seen and the sharpest, as though it had been shaved at the whetstone until it was a deadly perfection.

I tried to scramble out of reach of the weapon, but the tip ripped into the flesh on my lower leg. Blinding pain rushed through me, making the world spin.

I could see Gunnar frantically straining to shift the stone over the opening. His arms bulged and his veins pulsed as he hefted it upward again. Then he released his hold so that it slammed down upon the jotunn's head. The heavy pressure threw the jotunn off balance. He wavered but a second before he lost his grasp of the ladder and began to plummet.

As he fell, he clasped my boot. With surprising force, he dragged me with him.

Chapter 27

Karina

"No!" I seized Torvald around the waist to keep the jotunn from taking him down the hole.

The stone lid Gunnar was hefting into place slammed down onto Torvald, directly on the leg the jotunn was holding.

At what sounded like the crunching of bones, I cried out and hauled against Torvald harder.

A groan escaped through Torvald's tightly clenched teeth.

Gunnar gripped the stone and lifted it slightly. "Pull him free," he called to me.

I tugged Torvald with all my might. From the strain in his face and his ragged breathing, I sensed the pain he was experiencing. The ground around him was growing slick with his blood.

"He is bleeding too fast." I couldn't get a look at the injury due to the position of the stone lid and the darkness. But I suspected the jotunn had severed an artery, and that Torvald would bleed to death if I didn't tie off the flow.

"Is the jotunn still holding you?" Gunnar strained to keep the lid from falling again onto Torvald.

Torvald unsheathed his knife. Then with shaking fingers, he slid it down his leg, moving under the stone.

The jotunn's angry muffled shouts filtered out.

Torvald pressed his lips together and stretched lower. In the next instant, he jabbed at something. "Now," he called breathlessly. "Pull me out."

As Gunnar raised the stone covering several more inches, I strained to lift Torvald. At the same time, he shoved hard, pulling himself up. As soon as Torvald's leg was free, Gunnar let the stone drop into place. It fell with a resounding clang, almost as if a portal to the underworld had closed and could nevermore be opened. I prayed that was truly the case and that we wouldn't have to see the jotunn ever again.

As I lay gasping next to Torvald, urgency wrapped cold fingers around my heart. I hadn't been trained to doctor the sick or wounded the way some nuns were, but I was knowledgeable enough, and I knew we needed to help him soon, or we would lose him.

I scrambled up, tearing at the linen I'd already been unraveling. It came loose easily.

Gunnar crawled next to Torvald and skimmed his leg. "The wound is right here."

I wrapped the linen above the spot and then cinched it tight. "Is that better?"

Gunnar probed the open wound again. "It's still bleeding excessively."

Torvald's head lolled to the side, the sign he'd fallen into an unconscious state. I was grateful he was still alive and with us, but I guessed the pain had become too much to bear.

"Let's take him into the other cave where we can see better." Gunnar stood and began to drag his friend by the arms away from the hole and down the passageway. I picked up the chalice and followed.

As Gunnar laid Torvald out on the floor of the cave that had once belonged to Sven, the torch flickering in the wall holder revealed the extent of the damage to Torvald's leg. Not only was blood still pouring from a deep knife gash, his knee and the bones in his lower leg were compressed and misshapen.

At the sight of the damage, nausea rose swiftly within me. Even though I wanted to bend over and empty my stomach, I drew in a breath and touched my fingers against the pulse in Torvald's neck. His heart was still beating, but it was growing sluggish. Did we dare test the chalice and discover if it could heal? Or would we waste precious time doing so only to discover it didn't work?

Gunnar was already tearing more strips of cloth from his tunic. As fast as he ripped, I tied them around Torvald's wound, praying we could stanch the flow of blood.

Together we pressed hard against his leg until but a trickle remained. Finally, I sat back on my heels, my fingers coated with the blood of the man I loved. Only then did I realize I was shaking and that tears were covering my cheeks. "What do we do now?"

Wiping his hands onto his tunic, Gunnar rose. His expression was grave as he examined Torvald, who remained unmoving. "He's too injured to move. Doing so would surely be the death of him."

But would remaining in the cave prove equally fatal? I didn't know if we were truly safe from the jotunn. We didn't know how long we had before he made an attempt to push the stone lid off the hole. If he was able to free himself, he would soon be upon us, cursing and punishing us.

Gunnar paced several feet, then spun and paced again. "This is my fault. I should have been the one to attack the jotunn, not Torvald. Then I released the stone covering too soon and crushed his leg."

I reached for Torvald's hand and held it. "If anyone is to blame, I am the one. I rushed into the forest, hoping to spare Torvald. Instead of protecting him, I led him to greater danger. I shouldn't have interfered and should have allowed you to carry forth with your plans."

"No. I realize now we wouldn't have been able to get the chalice. Not without your aid."

"You would have figured out something." I couldn't allow Gunnar to bear the weight of this tragedy. He had so much of life ahead of him, especially with a beautiful woman who adored him.

Torvald and I, on the other hand, weren't destined to be together. "You must go and bring back help as swiftly as possible." We couldn't waste time arguing over who was at fault for the current predicament, not when Torvald's life was at risk. "I will stay with Torvald and care for him as best as I am able while you are gone."

Gunnar hesitated, glancing at the jotunn's chamber. "You're certain? The jotunn—"

"If he escapes, I will pull the thread out of the passageways so that you know not to come back inside unless you are prepared to face him." Both Torvald and I could very well perish. Nevertheless, I would do all I could to save the others from such fate.

"Torvald would want me to force you to go and escape this place while you can."

I stiffened. "I will not leave him. And you cannot make me do so."

Gunnar leaned his head against the cave wall, his shoulders slumping.

"Should we make Torvald drink from the chalice and see if it revives him?" I glanced to where I'd discarded it near the fire pit in my haste to help Torvald. The cup didn't appear to be anything special, not more so than any other chalice I'd seen.

"Sven told us that the jotunn drank from the chalice multiple times hoping to cure the pain in his bones and joints, but he was never healed. We've discussed the matter at length and have concluded that there is a secret to unlock the power of the chalice, though we know not what."

I sighed my frustration. Why had we put ourselves into such grave danger for a relic that was so mysterious? "You must take the chalice with you. We cannot let this encounter with the jotunn end in vain."

Gunnar crossed to the sacred relic, stared down at it, then at Torvald. "I will leave it here with you. If he worsens, you must try using it."

Selfishly, I longed to agree with Gunnar, but I also knew what Torvald would want—to ensure the chalice made it out of the forest and into the queen's hands. "'Tis for the queen—"

"I know Lis. And she would want Torvald to have it here . . . just in case."

I knew what he was inferring. That Torvald was at risk of losing his life. And I was better trying to use the chalice than letting Torvald perish. "If the jotunn escapes from his home, I shall do whatever I must to keep the chalice from falling back into his control."

Gunnar studied my face a moment longer before he nodded. "You are a good and kind woman, Lady Karina. I'll pray for a miracle, one that will save Torvald, you, and allow you both to find happiness together some day."

I wanted to confirm that we would indeed need a miracle, but I bit back the words and instead nodded my thanks.

Within seconds Gunnar was gone. When his pounding footsteps faded into nothing, I gathered Torvald's limp hand in mine again and pressed a kiss there. Love pulsed hard through my chest, rising into my throat and making it ache. I loved this man. And I didn't want him to die. Not today. And not because of me.

But what could I do except wait for help to arrive and pray the jotunn didn't have the strength to push the stone away from the hole?

Though I didn't want to leave Torvald's side, I followed the gleaming gold thread and returned to a spring of water I'd passed on my way in and gathered water into the blackened pot. With the few supplies I found in the cave, I washed his wound and applied fresh bandages whenever they became blood soaked. Through it all, Torvald remained unconscious. Even so, I plied sips of water into his mouth and forced the liquid down his throat.

All the while I worked, I kept one eye on the

passageway and the hole at the end where the jotunn was trapped. At every slight noise, I tensed, expecting the madman to appear but praying that he'd fallen to the depths below and would never return.

The chalice lay where I'd discarded it. The more I looked at it, the more the gleam of the gold drew me.

Finally, when I could no longer abide seeing it lying irreverently amidst the ashes, I crawled over and picked it up. Although I wanted to give Torvald a drink and see what might happen, I only needed to think of the tales regarding the Sword of the Magi to remind myself that holy relics could not be wielded at a whim.

As I examined the chalice, I released a gasp of horror. I was smearing blood all over the cup—Torvald's blood that remained on my hands. I had no wish to desecrate the sacred relic and began to set it back down. But then I froze. At the place where the prints of blood marred the gold, an engraving of ancient letters took shape, as if the blood was bringing them to life.

Was this a secret message of some kind carved into the gold, and had the blood revealed it?

I rubbed more of Torvald's blood over the cup, and as I did so, additional letters took shape. A tremor of anticipation coursed along my nerves.

I'd never enjoyed my Latin lessons at the convent, but I'd learned enough to discern that what I was seeing was indeed Latin. Slowly, I translated: *One can never gain something truly valuable without sacrifice.*

What did this mean? And why was it on the cup?

I twisted the stem. Was there more? On the opposite side of the chalice? Again, I brushed Torvald's blood over the gold.

A moment later, I was rewarded with another engraving: *With his stripes we are healed.*

I sat back on my heels and twisted the chalice around.

Both statements had to be the clues that helped the bearer understand the cup's ability to bring about healing, the secret to unlock the power of the chalice that no one yet knew.

What did it all mean?

With his stripes we are healed.

I recognized the second sentence as a Scripture verse. Although I couldn't exactly pinpoint where it was located, I knew it had to do with Christ. The stripes meant his blood. He'd sacrificed his blood to save humanity.

Perhaps the shedding of blood was necessary to bring about the desired healing. Torvald had shed his blood. Was that enough? Or must I sacrifice my blood too? Did the blood need to be consumed?

I shuddered at the thought of giving Torvald blood to drink. Even though barbaric, the process seemed too simple. The power of healing surely required more than that.

I fingered the Latin on the opposite side and re-read the words: *One can never gain something truly valuable without sacrifice.*

Sacrifice. That was it. A tiny thrill shot through me. The healing would require both sides of the cup, the blood and sacrifice. With the blood and a sacrifice, the cup would provide new life.

With the chalice, I returned to Torvald and took hold of his hand. It was limp and heavy. His eyes remained closed. And he was too still.

His condition seemed to be deteriorating. I had to try using the chalice to heal him. I couldn't tarry any longer. If I did, I might be too late.

Chapter 28

Karina

To save someone's life and bring them healing, surely I had to relinquish something of great value, something that would cost me dearly. What did I have to give?

I studied the cavern ceiling as if that could reveal the answer. The dark veins of black stone tangled with the reds and browns, the colors swirling in all different directions just like my choices. I could renounce my wealth. But that wouldn't truly be a sacrifice since it really belonged to my father. Besides, I didn't care about what I owned—would hand over my possessions to the poor if I could.

I could give up my future and freedom by returning to the convent. I'd lived there once and could do it again. *"I do not believe you were made for the convent, my lady."* Torvald's words pressed to the forefront of my memory. I hadn't wanted to admit he was right. But now that I'd had time away from the convent, I realized how stifled I'd been while living there. Surely if I was more suited for such a life, I wouldn't have needed to be beaten into silence so many times. Returning there would indeed be a sacrifice. But would it be enough?

Perhaps I could forsake my friends, including Marta? What about sacrificing my love of embroidery? Or perhaps I could vow never again to eat sweets.

I shook my head, frustration coursing through me. The truth was, everything was insignificant. Nothing mattered. I was a simple maiden with simple desires. Except for one thing... There was one thing—one person—that mattered far above anything else.

Torvald.

My body tightened in protest at the prospect of surrendering him. He was the only man I wanted, the only man I'd ever love. Yes, I'd overheard him say that he'd never allow himself to love me. But that didn't matter. I still loved him. Desperately. And even though I'd resigned myself to going to Finnmark with my family, I hadn't wanted to give up a hope and future with Torvald. Secretly, perhaps I'd been holding out hope that somehow, some way, he'd eventually find me worthy enough to love in return.

"I cannot give him up," I whispered even as the tears started to make a warm trail down my cheeks. "I do not think I can live without him."

As the words settled quietly around me, it became much too clear what I had to do. He was the only valuable treasure I had. If I sacrificed my connection with him, I would cause myself irreparable heartache. I might even kill a part of myself.

But in losing him, I would save him. Of that I was certain.

I used Torvald's knife to slice my palm. Then I

squeezed my fingers into a fist above the chalice and let my blood drip inside until I had enough for one small sip.

I lifted my heart heavenward and offered a prayer of sacrifice. "Though I do not want to release my aspirations for Torvald and earning his love, I give him up. I sacrifice him to you."

With my heartfelt words lingering in the air, I lifted Torvald's head as I'd been doing to give him sips of water. This time I placed the sacred chalice to his lips and tipped the scant few drops of my blood into his mouth. I made sure not even a drop dribbled out, and I was relieved to see his throat move in a reflexive swallow.

Had the sacred chalice healed him? I checked the rise and fall of his chest, the color of his skin, the pulse in his neck.

Nothing had changed . . . yet. Maybe the healing would take time. Maybe I had to be patient.

After a few moments, I laid his head back down. My fingers itched with the need to comb through his hair, to trail the scruff on his cheek, to brush across his lips. But I couldn't. I'd sacrificed my desire for him, and never again would I allow myself to touch him. Once he was out of the forest and back in the castle, I wouldn't allow myself to see him again either.

My gaze made a trail over his darkly handsome features, the tears flowing freely down my face and sadness swelling into every crevice of my body. I could give myself this one last look, one that would allow me to have a memory I could carry with me for the rest of my life. It would be all I had of him.

At an echoing shout and the pounding of footsteps,

I climbed to my feet, praying it was Gunnar and that he'd brought a physician with him. An instant later, he ducked into the chamber. His breathing came in gasps, and his face was perspiring, the sign that he'd run the whole way out and back without a break for himself.

His sights trained on Torvald. "Is he still alive?"

I nodded. "Yes."

Gunnar nodded and swallowed hard, his face taut with emotion. "Any sign of the jotunn?"

"No, the stone lid hasn't moved."

Before we could converse any further, more men poured into the room—all the Knights of Brethren, an unarmed man who was likely the physician, and even King Ansgar himself. As they crowded anxiously around Torvald and the physician knelt beside him, I handed the king the chalice, then I backed away.

I'd done all I could for the man I loved. Now it was time to follow through on the most difficult sacrifice I would ever make.

I trailed behind the stretcher with Torvald upon it, his knife wound now stitched and the several broken bones in his leg set back into place. Gunnar hoisted one end of the stretcher and Espen the other, with the king at his side carrying the chalice.

Everyone had remarked on my brilliance in leaving the golden thread as a guide. It had allowed Gunnar to safely make his way out of the confusing caves and dangerous forest. And it had enabled the knights to traverse the forest with all haste.

The king left behind several men to seal the stone that sat upon the hole. They also planned to close off the caves so that no one could ever go in or out again, with the hope that the jotunn would remain cut off from the world and never haunt Hardanger Forest again.

By the time we exited the forest, dawn had turned into bright daylight. News had spread that the jotunn had been trapped and was no longer a menace. People from all over Romsdal and the surrounding area had gathered. Their excited cheers and calls greeted us in the glory of a bright spring day.

We made our way into Likness Castle amidst the throngs. I wanted to follow Torvald to his chamber with the physician and make sure he was stable and recovering. But Maxim and Elinor along with the king and Sven asked to speak with me about the chalice, and I could do naught less than go to them and share all I'd discovered about the sacred relic, including the two hidden Latin engravings.

I held nothing back, telling them of my attempt to use the chalice to heal Torvald by blood and sacrifice. I assured them indeed I'd sacrificed what was most important to me. Thankfully, they didn't pry further into the nature of it.

After leaving their presence, Marta escorted me to a chamber near those of my family members. Once the door closed behind us, I fell into her arms and wept before giving myself over to an exhausted slumber.

When I awoke, I rolled over and opened my eyes to see long shadows. The day was nearly spent, which meant I'd slept for hours.

I pushed up, my hair tangling around me. I brushed

it aside to find Marta at my bedside, helping me to sit. "Torvald? How is he?"

From everything I'd gathered before he'd been rushed to his chamber, he'd been holding steady. He hadn't regained consciousness, nor had he deteriorated further. I'd taken hope that the chalice's healing powers had aided his recovery. If not, the physician's salves and ointments would surely save him.

"He's alive, my lady, but still in a great deal of pain from what I've been told." Marta pulled my hair away from my face, giving me a view of the lonely chamber, empty of everyone but the two of us.

What had I hoped for? Perhaps that my father would be waiting by my bedside, anxious for me to awaken so he could express his love and tell me how worried he'd been while I'd been gone? Or maybe I'd hoped to see Torvald miraculously recovered, sitting in the chair, ready to declare his love and tell me he couldn't live without me.

I released a sigh and flopped into my pillows. "His wounds are healing?"

"The king's own physician is tending to Torvald and is doing his best to ensure there are no long-term problems as a result of the broken bones."

Disappointment stabbed me. If the physician was still worried about Torvald, then it didn't appear the chalice had brought healing after all. Nevertheless, I aimed to keep the sacrifice I'd made just in case the promise of healing was a slow one that worked a more natural course. After all, it was possible that without the chalice, Torvald could have died there on the floor of the cave before getting the help he needed.

I had the sudden need to rush to his chamber and

see for myself how he fared. The urge was over-whelming, and I had to grasp the mattress beneath me to hold myself in place. I'd vowed to never touch or see him again. The only way I could do so was to put as much distance between us as I possibly could. I had to leave.

"When is my father returning to Finnmark?" Again, I pushed down the hurt that he wasn't by my side.

"He's waiting to discover what you would like to do."

"Would you take him the message that I shall be ready just as soon as the arrangements can be made. We could leave this eve if that is possible."

"I'll let him know."

"And the queen?"

Even as I asked, the door to my chamber swung open, and the queen glided inside, several ladies in waiting behind her, including the Princess Elinor. They wore elegant gowns with trains that trailed behind them. Silky veils swirled over the queen's reddish-blond hair and Elinor's long blond hair. As sisters they wore beautiful matching bangles.

Why had they come to visit me? With a racing heart, I scrambled to sit up again.

The queen put out a hand. "Please. Don't trouble yourself to rise."

I held myself motionless, stiff against my pillows, mortified to be abed, attired in a nightgown and my hair in tangles. "Your Majesty." I bowed my head as best I was able. "I am honored you would take the time to seek me out, although I feel as if I ought to rise, dress, and then visit you in your chambers."

The queen approached the bed, and only then did I

notice the tears streaking her cheeks. Her face was alight and her eyes happy, and I could only assume her tears were those of joy and not sadness.

I sucked in a breath of surprise—and mortification—when she knelt beside the bed. I motioned to Marta to offer a chair, but the queen reached for my hand, then brought it to her lips and kissed it.

When she lowered my hand and looked up at me, her vibrant green eyes—though filled with tears—held gratefulness. "Thank you, my lady."

Was she thanking me for helping find the chalice? Gunnar and Torvald deserved her thanks more than I did. They'd been the ones to orchestrate the attack against the jotunn and had risked their lives locking him away. "Your Majesty, I pray the chalice will bring you the healing that you seek."

She smiled then, a smile radiating with beauty and health and vitality.

A burst of excitement coursed through me. Maybe the chalice hadn't worked its healing power upon Torvald, at least not the way I'd believed it would, but clearly the queen was doing better in a much shorter time. "You drank from it and have already experienced its healing qualities."

"No, not quite." She began to rise, and her ladies were immediately at her side to aid her. But she waved them away and stood on her own. Her coloring was better, and she was clearly stronger. "I didn't drink from the chalice."

"But you look better."

"I stopped bleeding last night."

"Last night? I do not understand."

"We've concluded that the bleeding ceased about

the same time you locked the jotunn away."

My mind swirled with the news. "How?"

"Maxim and Elinor believe my curse was broken when the jotunn was sent back to the depths of the earth."

I didn't understand.

Seeing my confusion, she continued. "We have speculated that my family's curse originated from a jotunn, but we didn't know for certain. Now that the bleeding has stopped, we are more certain that it was so."

I'd already heard the tale about Queen Lis, that her mother Princess Blanche had suffered from the bleeding disease. Blanche had suspected it was a family curse that could be passed on to her firstborn daughter Lis. Hoping to spare her infant daughter, Blanche had run away and cut Lis off from her kin, which was why Lis had grown up on a remote Norvegian farm, not realizing she was royalty until just last autumn. Though Blanche had tried to find healing and break the curse, nothing had worked.

Until now. . . .

The queen's happiness was contagious, and I found myself smiling, overwhelmed with gratitude to God for the miracle given to this beautiful queen. It hadn't been the way we'd planned, but wasn't that the nature of miracles? They rarely came the way anyone expected.

"Thank you for your part in trapping the jotunn," the queen continued. "Without your bravery and your glowing golden thread, we wouldn't have ended the menace. And I wouldn't be standing here free of my family's disease."

I was thrilled for the queen that some good had come from my journey into Hardanger Forest. Even so, a heaviness weighed upon me—a heaviness from knowing that though we had defeated the jotunn, in the process I'd lost the best and most precious gift I'd ever been given.

Chapter 29

TORVALD

IF I HAD TO LIE ABED FOR ONE MORE HOUR WITHOUT SEEING Karina, I would go absolutely mad.

Where was she? And why hadn't she come to visit me?

Upon gaining consciousness, I'd expected her to be by my side, holding my hand and whispering encouraging words. I'd asked about her and learned she was unharmed and had returned to the castle with everyone. But over the course of the past three days, she'd not once stepped foot into my chamber.

I'd been heavily sedated with pain tonics and had slept most of the time. But today, I'd awoken and felt as though I could climb out of bed and join the king and his army. But the king had left for Vordinberg to prepare for King Canute's invasion.

He'd come to my chamber on several occasions to check on my well-being and to thank me for putting my life at risk in order to defeat the jotunn. The last time he'd visited, the queen had accompanied him. Together they'd presented me with a new title of honor, bequeathing upon me an earldom, additional lands, and a bag of gold and silver, enough that I could repair and save Wahlburg without taking Karina's dowry.

They'd done likewise for Gunnar. It was their way of thanking us for our gallant deeds. Although they'd wanted to give Karina the same gifts, Lord Royse had insisted he needed no more wealth, especially because word of Karina's use of the golden thread was spreading throughout the land, giving him the fame and respect he'd sought.

Karina. My beautiful and kind-hearted wife. She'd done everything with no thought to herself. Even now, she wasn't demanding anything in return for her heroism.

I turned restlessly in my bed, ready to get up. But the one time I'd tried earlier in the day, the physician as well as my squires had pushed me back. The physician had scolded me severely, reminding me of the damage I could do to my leg and the possibility of never walking again if I attempted anything too soon.

After having nearly lost my life in the fight against the jotunn, I was grateful to be alive and have my leg. In the cave, before falling into unconsciousness, I hadn't expected to keep my leg, had believed the bones were shattered. I'd been surprised to awaken to find my limb still attached to my body. I'd examined it, expecting it to be deformed and crushed. But it had been whole, the bones and muscles still working.

Even the slash from the jotunn's deadly knife hadn't been as deep as I'd first believed. The physician had apparently stitched it together before leaving the cave. By that point, it had already stopped bleeding, likely from the bindings Gunnar and Karina had tied to cut off the blood flow. Thankfully, the wound hadn't putrefied over the ensuing days. And the physician was pleased with how well it was healing.

I glanced at the closed door. Did I dare defy the physician and search for Karina? Or did I need to implore someone to fetch her?

The question from before haunted me again: Why hadn't she sought me out of her own accord? If she'd overheard my discussion with the king and my fellow Brethren, perhaps she was convinced I would never love her. But I was only fooling myself with such a declaration. The truth was what my friends had observed already. I was madly in love with my wife.

I'd known it in the cave as I'd been fighting the jotunn. I hadn't been doing it for the king and queen. I'd wanted to destroy the jotunn to protect Karina. I would have done anything for her. In fact, I'd been willing to die for her and her alone.

Even now, the power and passion of my feelings for her rocked through my body. I shifted my sights away from the door, my breathing shallow and my muscles taut. The intensity of the depth of my love for her frightened me more than the jotunn, more than King Canute, and even more than the Dark Warriors.

And I knew that was why I hadn't yet summoned her to my bedside. I was afraid.

I squeezed my eyes closed and drew in a steadying breath.

Espen's words from earlier in the week replayed inside my head: *Stop squandering the love she's offered you. Cherish every moment you have with her, for you don't know how many more moments you have left.*

As soon as my leg was strong enough, I intended to join the king and the army in the battle against King

Canute. Until then, I had to stop living in fear of the mistakes of my family.

Could I finally allow myself to believe I was different? She was different? And that our love was destined to be different?

I rolled to my back and stared up at the canopy. All I could see was her beautiful face, the freckles across her nose, her perfectly kissable mouth, and her bewitching red hair.

I groaned and then pushed myself up so that I was sitting.

"My lord?" The physician rose from his seat beside the bed where he'd been dozing. "What ails you?"

One of my squires was at the foot of my bed in the next instant as well, watching, waiting, wanting to be useful.

But their hovering only irritated me. I was fine. I didn't want their help. All I wanted was Karina. Suddenly I needed to behold her more than I needed to breathe. "Fetch my wife."

My squire's brows rose. "Fetch your wife?"

"Yes. Anon."

"But, my lord . . ." the squire started, then stopped before exchanging a glance with one of the other squires.

Something in their faces set me on edge. Had ill befallen Karina? Had she been hurt after all? Perhaps the physician had ordered the news be kept from me so that it wouldn't upset me and undo his efforts to bring about my healing.

A new sense of urgency prodded me. I kicked off my covers and swung my legs over the side of the bed.

"My lord, please." The physician laid a hand against my shoulder. "You cannot get out of bed."

I didn't care. I was going to find Karina, and that was all there was to it. I lurched to my feet, and pain shot through my injured leg. I grabbed onto the chair to keep from collapsing.

"Your leg is unable to bear weight yet." The physician attempted to guide me back to the bed.

I shrugged off his hold and braced myself against the wall. Already I was breathless from the throbbing. But I pushed several more steps toward the door only to realize I was attired in my breeches. I couldn't go to Karina without first getting dressed.

"Bring me my clothing." I motioned to my squires. My leg burned, but it wasn't nearly as bad as I'd expected.

They hesitated.

"I intend to see my wife."

The squire at the end of my bed cleared his throat. "She is no longer in Romsdal."

I froze, one hand still on the wall. "Where is she?"

"She left with her kin for Finnmark two days ago."

Two days ago? Without saying farewell? "Why did no one tell me?"

The squire cleared his throat again, fidgeted with his doublet, then peered at one of the others as though asking for help.

Another of the men stepped forward. "My lord, we assumed you were already aware of her departure."

I leaned my shoulder against the wall, my weakness making me dizzy. Why hadn't she come to visit me? To wish me well? At the very least, to inform me of her plans?

Even when I'd left Wahlburg that morn with Espen, she'd rushed down to see me off. I hadn't given her any reason to do so, and still she'd wanted to say good-bye.

Had she grown so disillusioned with me and my pushing her away that she'd decided she'd had enough?

I couldn't blame her. I was at fault for not cherishing her the way she deserved. And I'd been the one to tell her to go with her father to Finnmark. Yes, I'd wanted her in a safe place. But I'd also done so to protect myself against getting too close to her.

The physician tucked his hand into my arm, and this time I let him lead me back to the bed, limping as I did so, my leg aching but not nearly as badly as my heart.

As he helped me sit, I perched on the wooden bed box. "Did she leave me any word?" I was hungry for some indication she'd thought of me, even if only a little.

My squires again shifted, clearly nervous.

The warring inside me tapered to an eerie hum. They knew something I did not—something I didn't want to hear, something that would deliver a fatal blow.

I stiffened my shoulders. I was a courageous man. I'd faced violent Ice Men, fire-breathing red dracos, and even a cursing jotunn. I could face this news regarding Karina. "I give you leave to speak the truth."

"My lord." The squire at the end of the bed spoke first. "We do not know much. But we have heard that before leaving she requested an annulment of your marriage and has decided to return to the convent and become a nun."

Annulment. The word pummeled into me with the force of a battering ram. Karina had asked for an annulment. And she wanted to return to the convent.

For a long moment, I could only sit in stunned silence. But then as the realization of what she'd done hit me, I buried my face in my hands. If she'd wanted me, even just a little, why had she rejected me so completely? Why ask for an annulment?

Clearly, her feelings for me had been fickle, had faded at the first sign of adversity. Instead of speaking with me and telling me the truth, she'd severed our relationship and sailed away without a warning or explanation. Just like my mother had done to my father. My mother hadn't said good-bye to my father or me. She'd disappeared without a word. And she'd never contacted us again.

I'd been foolish to allow myself to even think about the possibility of having a real marriage and of permitting myself to love Karina without anything holding me back.

All along I'd known I was doomed to love too deeply, too passionately, too whole-heartedly. And now, the burning in my chest told me I'd done exactly what I'd hoped to avoid. I'd fallen in love with a woman, had given her my heart—even though I'd tried not to—and she'd crushed it and crushed me.

But even as anger and frustration burned through me, so did desire for her. I couldn't imagine waking up every day to a life without Karina in it. I couldn't imagine not touching or kissing her again. I couldn't imagine not seeing her smile and the happiness filling her eyes.

I wanted to cry out at the empty ache where my heart had once resided. I also wanted to fall back into my mattress, bury myself under my covers, and find a way to avoid reality and my life without her.

Was that what had happened to my father? Had he given in to this despair? Had he felt this same way, that he never wanted to wake up to a day without his wife?

At the image of him wasting away in his bed, bitterness swelled up, filling my chest and pushing out the pain of Karina's rejection.

Maybe I'd been a fool to fall for a woman the same way my father had. But I didn't have to continue down the same path and let this love for a woman dictate the rest of my life. Instead, I had to eliminate her from my thoughts, banish my love for her, and proceed with renewed purpose in serving the king and my country.

If only I had the will and the strength to do so.

Chapter 30

Torvald

I LIMPED ALONG THE PASSAGEWAY WITH MY CANE.

After practicing walking in my chamber for the past two days and strengthening my leg, I'd deemed myself sturdy enough to make the longer trek. Of course, the physician had objected to my regimen. He'd been under strict orders from the king to do everything within his power to keep me from taxing myself too soon.

I assured him I would excuse him from any repercussions for my actions. He wasn't to blame for my unwillingness to heed his advice. And I would make sure the king knew my damage was due to my own obstinacy.

The truth was, my leg was healing faster than any of us had expected. With each passing hour of walking and stretching, I could feel the strength returning.

With the news earlier in the morn that a party of Dark Warriors had been spotted crossing the border into Norvegia, I wanted to ride to Vordinberg and be with the king and the army as they prepared to push King Canute back into Swaine.

I wasn't ready yet. But within another day, I intended to leave.

Passing by the door to the great hall, a voice from within called to me. "My lord, good to see you recovering so quickly." Sven stepped into the passageway and into my path.

I halted and tamped down my irritation at being stopped. I could admit my mood had been dismal since learning of Karina's departure. In fact, my mood had been outright incorrigible. I loathed talking with anyone. And didn't want anyone speaking to me.

Though I'd tried to forget about Karina, all I'd done was think about her. I hated myself for my weakness. But at least I'd been able to force myself out of my bed—unlike my father.

Sven studied my injured leg, the bandages visible beneath my hose. "I see that the healing quality of the sacred chalice is working after all."

"I have not been healed by the chalice." I narrowed my eyes upon him. "You do not know of what you speak."

"I was present with Lady Karina when she explained to the king as well as Maxim and Princess Elinor what she did to save you with the chalice."

A strange disquiet stole through me. Was the chalice to account for why I hadn't died? And for why my injuries were healing so rapidly? "What did she do?"

Sven peered at me intently, as though seeing the turmoil inside me. "She discovered hidden writing on the cup, explaining that healing could happen through blood and sacrifice."

Blood and sacrifice? Had she hurt herself on my account? I lifted a brow and waited for Sven to explain further.

"She gave you a sip of her blood."

I tensed, loathing the thought that she'd sliced her own flesh. "And her sacrifice?"

"She did not reveal it to us. But I think it is quite clear."

It wasn't clear to me.

As if sensing my confusion, Sven continued. "Sacrifice must oft come at a great cost and entail giving up something that means everything."

What meant everything to Karina?

"You," Sven said softly, as though he'd heard my unspoken question.

I shook my head, a stone settling in my stomach.

"She loved you, my lord. I beheld the despair upon her countenance as she left the castle."

Feeling suddenly weak, I clutched my cane tighter, leaning upon it heavily. Was I relieved? That she hadn't rejected me?

Even as the emotion circled through me, I cut it off. What kind of selfish imbecile was I to find relief in this situation? She'd sacrificed her future for me. She didn't belong in a convent. I'd realized that the first time I'd met her.

"I cannot let her make such a sacrifice."

"She already has."

I straightened, glancing around for an answer, anything to free Karina from her obligation. I didn't know enough about the chalice, but surely I could find a way to revoke her sacrifice. "I would rather suffer than have her give up so much."

The half of Sven's face that wasn't scarred turned up in a smile. "Perhaps you will find a way to sacrifice for her."

"Will that free her from her obligation to me?"

"None of us truly know how miracles happen. But I suspect Providence works them out in the ways he determines are best."

Even if I couldn't free her, I needed to try. Of that I was certain. What I didn't know was whether I was worthy of a woman like Karina. She'd loved me even when I hadn't given her any hope of returning my love. She'd gone into the forest to face the jotunn to save me from having to do so. And when I'd lain dying on the cave floor, she'd given up her freedom to bring me new life.

I wasn't worthy of her. But I wanted to be. Was there still hope I could become a man who was capable of loving selflessly and unconditionally?

Before that could happen, I suspected I had some work to do first. And I knew where I needed to start.

The ride was long and hard. Although my leg pained me, I pushed onward regardless. After Sven's revelation, now 'twas clear why I was able to do the impossible.

As my squires and I ascended the trail from the river bottoms and the walls of Wahlburg Castle came into view, I reined back in surprise at the sight of laborers repairing the fortifications.

Who had ordered the work? And why? Perhaps Ingold had learned of the Dark Warriors entering Norvegia and wanted to be prepared.

Whatever the case, I was relieved for the foresight. I just hoped the most needed reparations could be made in time.

As we reached the gatehouse, I was surprised again to

see people coming and going, bringing in supplies of food, fuel, and weapons. From what I could assess, Wahlburg was preparing for a siege.

At the sight of me, the guards on duty bowed in respect and the laborers halted to watch me pass. I rode directly to the keep, dismounted, and then hobbled up the steps as fast as my stiff leg would allow.

I pushed open the door and shuffled inside. "Ingold?"

A manservant appeared in the doorway of the great hall, his brow lifting in surprise. "My lord?"

I pressed onward down the passageway that led to my father's chambers, my cane tapping a determined rhythm. "Tell Ingold to meet me at my father's chambers anon."

"I cannot do that, my lord." The servant's timid response halted me.

With a glare, I spun.

"I cannot because Ingold is no longer at Wahlburg."

My retort stalled.

"Your father dismissed him."

I realized my mouth was ajar and quickly clamped it closed. Why had my father sent Ingold away? Had he lost his mind completely now?

As if seeing the questions in my eyes, the manservant continued his explanation. "After Lord Royse's investigation, your father discovered Ingold was cheating on the ledgers and setting aside the profits for his own coffers."

Ingold? He'd served for so many years, had seemed faithful. But perhaps he'd seen the weakness in my father and had been taking advantage of him all along.

With even heavier steps, I resumed my limping stride toward my father's room.

"If you'd like to see your father," the servant called, "he's in the antechamber."

This time I stumbled to a stop. My father was out of bed? Yes, he'd attended my wedding to Karina. But beyond that, I couldn't remember the last time he'd arisen from bed, much less visited his antechamber.

"You are certain?" I recognized this manservant as one who had attended my father for many years, but I regretted I didn't recall his name.

He bowed his head. When he lifted his face, his eyes were alight with hope, a hope that stirred something inside me.

I retraced my steps, then passed the servant into the great hall, which was a bustle of activity as servants and many other people—likely tenants—worked together plucking feathers, dressing game, preparing berries, and more.

"He'll be glad to see you, my lord." The man followed behind me as I made my way through the busy room. I garnered plenty of stares as I passed, and conversations came to a halt, but at least everyone kept working this time.

As I reached the antechamber, I was winded, my body aching and exhausted. The punishing ride to Wahlburg was taking its toll. But before I rested, I needed to finish what I'd come to do.

Without knocking, I pushed open the door.

Sitting at his desk, my father didn't look up from a ledger he was poring over. Two burly men stood on either side of him. Their wide-brimmed straw hats, as well as their long woolen tunics, distinguished them as shepherds. At the sight of me, they stood straighter, their expressions registering recognition and respect.

"Any news on the Dark Warriors, Rubart?" my father asked.

Behind me, the manservant—Rubart—pushed forward. "Your son is here, my lord."

My father scooted back from his desk and was on his feet in an instant. Although he was still emaciated and his clothing hung from his frame, a new energy emanated from him, one of purpose. "Torvald? What are you doing here? I sent your wife and her kin to safety days ago."

"Yes, I know. I saw them in Romsdal before they left for home." I guessed the news of my injury and finding the chalice hadn't yet reached Wahlburg. I would have time later to explain all of that to my father. But at this moment, I needed to speak my piece before I lost my courage.

"Is she safe?" The flash of anxiety in my father's eyes told me he already loved Karina like a daughter. How would he take the news that I'd lost her? Would it devastate him again?

"Yes, by the grace of God." I still inwardly trembled every time I thought about how close she'd been to the jotunn. God's grace had saved her from being hurt or cursed. And her kindness, sweetness, and beauty had all helped too, all traits the jotunn had been unable to resist—traits no one could resist.

"What is it, then?" Father remained standing behind his desk.

I glanced between the two shepherds, who were watching our exchange with open curiosity.

Father nodded at them. "Would you please give me a moment with my son? We will carry on later."

They murmured their assent and exited, closing the door firmly, leaving silence in their wake.

Father gripped the back of his chair so tightly his knuckles turned white.

During the ride to Wahlburg, I'd rehearsed what I needed to say. But now, faced with this man I'd regarded with anger and frustration for so many years, the words stuck someplace deep inside.

He stared down at the ledgers open upon his desk, and the muscles in his jaw twitched. Did he have something he wanted to say to me too?

I had to do this. It's why I'd come. "I forgive you."

The words fell out. Not what I'd planned. Not what I'd wanted to say. But they were all that was necessary. I'd let my bitterness toward him fester and make me weaker. If I let it go, I'd finally be able to move on without the heaviness of the past keeping me from truly living—and loving.

My father nodded, his throat working up and down in a hard swallow.

"'Tis past time for me to stop holding on to everything that happened . . . with Mother." I drew in a breath, feeling lighter for having said what I needed, as if the burdens had been cut loose.

"'Tis past time for me to stop holding on too." My father's voice was so soft I wondered if I'd heard him correctly.

He was silent and stared at his desk a moment longer before lifting his eyes to mine. "I have many regrets. The worst is seeing your fear of loving Karina and knowing I caused it."

His confession pummeled into me, weakening me so that I had to lean against my cane lest I lose my balance. I hadn't expected his reaction. In fact, I hadn't expected any of this—him to be out of bed in his office managing his affairs. Something had changed in him, and I knew who was responsible. Karina. She had a way of bringing out the best in people because she only saw the best in them. Just another reason I loved her.

I didn't know how to respond, so I said nothing.

He slipped his hand inside his shirt and pulled out the chain with Mother's ring. Then in a swift jerk, he broke it from his neck. He strode to the open window and tossed the necklace out into the ravine below. Without a backward glance, he returned to his desk. "I should have done that long ago, and I regret I did not."

It was never too late to start over, was it? I wanted to assure him he was doing the right thing, but the words stuck in my throat.

"Please do not let fear hold you back any longer from loving her." His eyes welled with tears.

"I may not be the man she deserves." I couldn't remember the last time I'd spoken so honestly with my father, perhaps never. I shuffled awkwardly, unsure of the nature of our relationship moving forward. I didn't know if we'd ever be able to repair all that had been broken. Human nature wasn't as easily mended as bricks and mortar. Nevertheless, I would pray for a better future.

"I poured myself out for your mother until I was empty. She could not give anything back the way I expected and wanted. Instead of finding strength in Providence to carry on, I let weakness overtake me."

His explanation seemed to loosen another knot tying me to my past, one I hadn't known was binding me.

"But Karina . . . she has proven she will give everything."

My father was right. Karina was nothing like my mother. She was always giving a measureless amount to all those around her without thought to herself.

"Now you must do so too. Then you and Karina—you will enrich each other."

I wouldn't argue with my father about Karina enriching me. But I'd yet to learn how to enrich her. I just prayed I would yet have one last chance to show her that I treasured her more than anything else.

Chapter 31

Karina

I'd been back at the convent for only one week, but it already felt like an eternity.

I tucked my hands deeper into my wide sleeves and kept my head bowed as I traversed as quietly as I could along the passageway.

A message from the abbess had drawn me out of the garden where some of us had been silently embroidering and attempting to enjoy the beauty of the June afternoon. I admit I hadn't been invested in either my embroidery or the beauty of the lush greens and blossoming flowers. But I'd persisted, hoping the activity would distract me from thoughts of Torvald.

The abbess had requested I return to my cell, and that usually meant only one thing. I was in need of punishment for some infraction or another, although I knew not what. Had I spoken overmuch? Perhaps smiled or laughed when I shouldn't have? What if I'd neglected one of my duties? Or had someone heard me crying into my pallet last night and reported me?

Chills prickled up my spine, and the bruises from my beating from several days ago suddenly ached unbearably.

My steps slowed the closer I drew to the small room I shared with Marta, the home that would now be mine for the rest of my life. The abbess and the convent had been surprised to see me when I'd shown up the day our ship landed in Finnmark. But they'd easily accepted my father's generous payment, taking me and assuring him they would take good care of me.

My father hadn't questioned my decision to return. Likely one place was the same as another to him. The truth was, I couldn't rely upon him. I never had been able to.

Though everyone else in my life might leave or forsake me, Providence never would. I had to remember that. If only I could do so more readily.

I sighed. Perhaps it was a truth that I would be struggling to accept the rest of my life.

In the late afternoon, the shadows in the passageway had grown darker, and I fought a shudder from the dampness emanating off the bricks. How had I ever thought I belonged to this place instead of out in the world, truly serving people in every capacity and at every turn?

Had I been too rash in coming back? I could have stayed with my father in his house, except that there I'd have a chance at some point of seeing Torvald.

I couldn't allow that to ever happen. I couldn't risk seeing or touching him and breaking the sacrificial vow I'd made and chance him facing death again.

I'd reminded myself of that very thing over and over, trying to convince myself I'd done what was right in letting him go and giving him the annulment. It would hurt him just a little—perhaps hurt his pride most of all. But he would soon put our short marriage behind him and move on. He no longer needed my money to save Wahlburg after receiving the king and queen's reward. He would be able to make his way in his own right.

With my steps at a crawl as I neared my door, I offered another prayer—for the king and queen and the rest of the knights who were preparing for the biggest battle Norvegia had ever faced. The throne and the future of the country was in jeopardy. I had no doubt that Torvald would be in the middle of the fighting once it commenced. Although I hadn't heard how he was faring recently, when I'd left Romsdal, the physician had reassured me he was healing well.

I placed a hand on my door, then took a deep breath, bent my head in submission to the abbess, and pushed my way into the room.

With my gaze trained upon the floor, I was confused by the sight of golden flowers strewn over every inch of the bare stone. My gaze jerked upward only to find vase after vase filled to overflowing with every imaginable golden flower that grew in Norvegia—dahlia, yarrow, tulips, goldenrod, loosestrife, and more I couldn't name.

Not only were there flowers, but my pallet was covered with a golden coverlet. A golden gown hung from the peg in the wall with a golden necklace dangling from the bodice. A golden candelabra sat upon the bedstead table with a golden bowl filled with more golden flowers.

Was I dreaming? I stepped farther into my chamber

and blinked hard.

I took it all in again, a sense of wonder spilling through me. I crossed to the nearest vase, buried my face in the flowers, and breathed in the sweet scent. What did all of this mean?

The door clicked closed, and I sensed an intense, masculine presence behind me, one that belonged to the man I most wanted but couldn't have. Torvald.

I froze. What was he doing here? He wasn't allowed in the convent. No men were.

But clearly, he'd done all of this. For me.

My throat closed up with an overwhelming love and longing for him. He'd remembered everything I liked, all the things I'd told him that day in the chapel when we'd first spoken—when he'd assumed I was a maid. No one had ever done anything like this for me before.

"Thank you, Torvald." I pressed my face into the nearest bouquet, letting the silky petals soothe the heat from my cheeks. "This is beautiful, everything. Glorious, really. I am absolutely astounded and amazed and—"

He grazed my veil, cutting off my words. He'd moved directly behind me, and his presence was even more overwhelming, especially as he pushed aside my wimple and tugged it off my head.

As it fluttered to the floor and pooled among the flowers, my pulse pattered with a strange anticipation. When his fingers began to loosen the leather tie at the bottom of my braid, I couldn't utter a word of protest. Instead, I closed my eyes and held my breath, letting him unravel the strands until my hair hung unfettered down my back.

I knew I should stop him. This interaction between us was completely inappropriate here, now. But I was helpless to resist.

He combed his fingers once through my hair, then held a fistful with a tension that radiated his passion.

I couldn't keep from sucking in a breath. Saints and angels, I'd missed him. How had I lived without him?

"Karina," he whispered, the longing in his voice stirring warmth in my belly. "Will you forgive me?"

"For what?" I whispered back.

"For not loving you the way I should have."

I drew in another breath. "You gave me what you could—"

"I held back. And I shall never do so again."

My pulse skipped. What was he saying?

"Henceforth, I give you my whole heart, soul, and body."

A deep trembling worked its way from my heart through my limbs. This was more than I'd ever imagined or dreamed of getting from Torvald. It was beyond my wildest expectations. And the sincerity in his voice told me he meant every word.

His fingers in my hair tightened. I wanted naught more than to lean back against him and feel the strength of his body. But I couldn't... I had to remember the sacrificial vow I'd made in the jotunn's cave—the vow that I wouldn't look at him or touch him ever again.

"I do not deserve the love of a woman like you." His voice turned hoarse, and I could only guess what it must cost him to open himself up and speak with such vulnerability. "But I vow to be worthy, and I shall love you to my dying breath."

Hot tears sprang to my eyes, and though I tried to squeeze them back, they began to spill over anyway. A heart-wrenching sob pushed up into my throat. Torvald was finally ready to love me unreservedly. As much as I wanted to give in to that love, I couldn't. I wouldn't take back the sacrifice I'd made and risk bringing him harm.

"I shall love you to my dying breath, also, my lord." I couldn't keep the anguish from punctuating each word. "But I have already signed the annulment."

He released his hold on me, and I nearly crumpled to the ground in my despair and in my desire to have his hands back upon me.

In the next instant, he thrust a paper in front of me. The petition of annulment. His signature was absent at the bottom. Before I could say anything, he rent it in half violently. Then he tore it again and again. When he could rip it no further, he released the final shreds from his hands and let them fall to the floor.

I could only stare at the pieces among the flowers.

"That is what I think of your annulment." His tone was harsh. "I shall never allow it."

The sob in my throat escaped, and I cupped a hand over my mouth to keep the rest at bay. This was all too late, and there was nothing we could do to be together.

I could feel the anger and frustration radiating from him. But a moment later, he swept aside my hair, laying my neck bare. Then he bent in and pressed his lips to the sensitive spot below my ear. At the warmth and softness of his mouth, I couldn't hold back a gasp. But at the same time, I took a rapid step away from him, making sure to keep my back facing him, lest I look upon him and cause him harm.

"Please, Karina . . ." His voice broke. "Let me prove I am a changed man."

"You need not prove anything, my lord. I love you for who you are and always will."

"Then what can I do to convince you to give me a second chance?"

Swiping unsuccessfully at the tears upon my cheeks, I swallowed past the ache in my throat. "It is too late, Torvald."

Before I knew what he was doing, he spun me around.

I cried out and averted my face. "I cannot look at you, my lord. Or touch you." I clasped my hands together so that I wouldn't accidentally touch him.

He held my upper arms to keep me in place.

I could only pray that his touching me wouldn't break the rules, since I wasn't initiating it.

He stood silently, his grip tight.

Being this close to him and hearing his beautiful declarations of love was rendering me weak. I had to make him leave before I gave in to my desire to feast upon him with both my eyes and hands.

"You sacrificed being married to heal me." His statement was so certain that I knew he'd figured out what had happened with the chalice.

"Yes." It wasn't as though I was hiding it from everyone. Maybe I hadn't shared all the personal details, but I'd been honest about using the chalice to aid Torvald. "When I realized my sacrifice could keep you alive, I had to do it. I had nothing else I could give that meant as much to me as you."

His fingers against my arms turned gentler. "You traversed the forest and faced the jotunn so I wouldn't have to. You offered to stay forever with the jotunn in exchange for the chalice. You remained with me in the cave instead of saving yourself. You've sacrificed more than was necessary already."

A tiny sprig of hope inside began to blossom. Maybe my willingness to go into the forest and face the jotunn was all that was required of me. "I would like to believe you are right, my lord. But what if I touch you or look at you and then you perish?"

"And what if I do not?"

"I cannot risk it."

Silence settled around us. Clasping my hands tightly, I kept my focus well away from him, looking at the ground.

"Karina?" He finally touched his fingers under my chin as though to force my head up.

I twisted away. "Do not make me do this. I will not put you in peril so that I might have a few hours or days of loving you."

"I would take a few hours or days of loving you than none at all."

Again, tears slipped out and streaked my cheeks. I shook my head. "No. Please, Torvald."

"Yes. I will not allow fear to hold me back from loving. Not in this. Not in anything." He bent in and angled his head, nuzzling my exposed neck with his nose before dropping a kiss there that was nearly my undoing.

"You enrich me," he whispered as he placed another kiss upon my neck. "Without you, I am naught."

For too long I'd lived in the shadows of others, so much that I'd forgotten my own worth. Maybe it was time to stop seeing the flaws in myself and instead recognize my value and the richness I could bring to others.

He lifted away from me just slightly, enough that I knew he was giving me this choice. He'd made his wishes known, but he wouldn't force himself upon me—although I could sense he wanted to.

I pinched my eyes closed and fought back a wave of anxiety. What if I made the wrong decision and Torvald died? But what if I didn't choose him, and we lost out on the chance to love each other, even if for just a short time?

Drawing in a deep breath, I tentatively turned my face toward his.

He didn't move.

I shifted again, nearer. My husband, the man I loved, was standing before me giving me everything. How could I turn away from that?

He slid his hand to my hair again, twining his fingers into the locks.

I loved when he took possession of me in that way. How could I not do likewise to him and cherish him for as long as we both had breath?

Throwing aside caution, I found his mouth and connected my lips with his. He responded gently, as though making sure I was certain. I pressed into him with more passion, giving him my answer.

That was all he needed to unleash the power he'd been holding back. His arms swept around me, crushing me while his kiss deepened into a summer storm of desire, the lightning streaking between us and the thunder booming inside my chest.

At the creak of my chamber door, I jerked away,

reality drawing me back into the convent and the fact that I was standing in my cell with a man.

Marta's face peeked through the door, and at the wide smile on her face, I guessed she'd been the one to help Torvald with his winning display of gold. As she quietly closed the door to allow us privacy, I let myself feast upon Torvald's handsome face, one I'd never expected to behold again.

He was doing the same to my face, hungrily taking in every detail. As he finished, he cupped both of his palms to my cheeks, framing my face, and then he bent in and kissed me again, his kiss assuring me that this was only the beginning of a lifetime of treasure together.

Chapter 32

TORVALD

THE ROUND TABLE WAS FULL. THE KING AND ALL THE OTHER Knights of Brethren crowded together, the prospect of war with Swaine uppermost on our minds. Almost uppermost . . .

Though I worried about the upcoming battle against King Canute and his Dark Warriors, I could admit Karina occupied most of my waking thoughts and had since I'd reunited with her in the convent six days ago. After I'd released her from the convent and after she'd had Marta help her pack up every single golden flower and gift I'd placed in her room, we'd spent several blissful days together at her father's home in Finnmark.

I hadn't wanted to leave, had simply wanted to bask in our love and in spending endless hours together. But with word of the Dark Warriors beginning to launch attacks in the black of the night, I'd known I had to voyage to the king's side and aid him in defeating the threat.

I was certain my wound was already mostly healed. In less than a fortnight since facing the jotunn, the pain was gone, the gash was but a red mark, and my strength was at full capacity. I was ready to rejoin the king and his army in the upcoming battle.

As much as I'd wanted Karina to stay behind where she could be safe and away from any danger, she'd pleaded to come with me, and I hadn't been able to resist, had actually been unable to fathom being apart from her.

Even now, I relished the prospect of finishing this meeting, finding Karina, and pulling her into my arms—my favorite place for her to be. Thankfully, she didn't protest how oft I held her. From the way she always came right to me, I hoped her favorite place was in my arms too.

"Isn't that right, Torvald?" Gunnar asked.

The question prodded me, and I tried to bring my focus back to the discussion. I sat forward and narrowed my gaze, pretending I was thinking about my answer.

Beside me, Espen elbowed me and grinned. "You have no idea what we're talking about, do you?"

The others were grinning at me too.

I glared at Espen and then around at the rest of my companions. "We are discussing how to keep the Dark Warriors from extinguishing our torches."

They laughed.

I'd obviously gotten my answer wrong. The Dark Warriors had perfected the ability to snuff out lights, so that no matter how many torches were lit, the warriors always brought about complete darkness anyway and then attacked, ruthlessly and mercilessly.

Kristoffer was the first to wipe away his humor. As a firstborn son of a wealthy nobleman, he'd been raised just as I had to one day rule his lands. Even though we were alike in that way, we were as different as high mountain and seaside.

Kristoffer was everything I was not—cultured, well-spoken, polite, and a politician. With his sensible and logical arguments, he could oft turn the staunchest of souls to his side.

Even now, his eyes contained a keenness that most men didn't have. "If Maxim and Princess Elinor have discovered that the holy lamp might give us an advantage over the Dark Warriors, then we must seek this relic."

Espen exchanged a glance with Kristoffer, one that told me the two had already discussed the issue. "Since Gunnar and Torvald went on a quest for the chalice, Kristoffer and I humbly beseech the king to send us to look for the lamp."

King Ansgar's mouth was set in grim determination. "We must find the lamp with all haste. I suggest we send two teams. Espen you'll lead one, and Kristoffer will lead the other. You'll need to confer with Maxim and Princess Elinor regarding where to start your search. In the meantime, I've sent out couriers to warn people who live near the valley to take refuge and to reinforce the fortresses in the vicinity."

From the latest news our scouts had delivered, we'd learned King Canute's army wasn't yet amassed at the border, that so far only Dark Warriors had entered the country. Even so, King Ansgar had sent word throughout Norvegia of the need for troops. Knights with their foot soldiers were arriving every day and preparing to march out to the Valley of Red Dragons for another battle against King Canute.

The trouble was that we had yet to discover a way to combat the Dark Warriors. Currently the best option appeared to be the holy lamp, which Maxim and Elinor believed couldn't be extinguished by normal means and would somehow provide the light we needed to see our enemies. Without light, everyone had concurred, we would only be sending our men out to be slaughtered. Thus, we'd agreed to wait as long as possible before leaving the safety of Vordinberg, praying we would find the holy lamp to aid us first.

The wait was perfectly fine with me. I pushed away from the table and stood, drawing the attention of every man present again.

Too late I realized the king hadn't dismissed us.

The meeting was nearly finished anyway. There wasn't much more we could do now. And I wanted to spend the days before the battle with Karina.

Even so, I bowed my head respectfully toward the king, ignoring his amused expression and raised brow. "Your Majesty, please excuse me. I am feeling the need to rest."

The king's brow arched higher, and the others broke out into guffaws.

"Aye, *rest*." Espen winked. "To be sure."

I tossed him a glower, but my insides heated with embarrassment that my friends could so easily detect my eagerness to be with Karina.

"Methinks we should all adjourn." Gunnar rose with a wide grin. "I'm due for a *rest* now as well. Aren't you too, Ansgar?"

The king nodded and pretended to yawn. "Yes, I think you're right."

Kristoffer shook his head as though we'd all gone mad. Perhaps we had, over our wives.

"What do you think, Kris?" Espen asked. "Do you think we'll have the same good fortune as our friends? If they could find true love while on their quests, what are the chances that we will also find love?"

"The probability is unlikely." Kristoffer spoke as seriously as always. "With so much at stake, we cannot allow ourselves to get distracted by women."

Although Kristoffer didn't address me specifically, I guessed I was his main target. After all, I'd been the one distracted all throughout the meeting. As it was, I didn't care what Kristoffer thought of me, didn't care if he believed I was lovesick. I wanted Karina. And I'd been apart from her long enough for the day.

With a final nod to the king, I strode from the room, heedless of any further comments or looks. I knew where I'd find my wife. And I was right. She was down in the castle kitchen and storerooms, preparing for her daily distribution to the poor, filling baskets with leftovers.

As I approached the storeroom, the several servants working with her scurried away. I didn't mind that my presence intimidated them. If it allowed me time alone with Karina, then all the better.

I tried to sneak up behind her, but she spun and raced to me, throwing her arms around my neck and pulling me down into a kiss—a bottomless one where I was sinking and never again wanted to come up for breath.

But as quickly as she began the kiss, she ended it, pulled back, and smiled at me with her contagious joy. "I missed you."

"I was gone but an hour."

Her lashes fell and her cheeks turned pink. "It was an hour too long, my lord."

I tugged her against me, wrapping my arms around her, embracing her as fully as I could. This was where I wanted her. Always. "It was an hour too long for me also."

"Good." She snuggled against me. "You are feeling well?"

"Yes. Better than ever before." I knew she still worried about my health and whether or not I would get sick as a result of us being together. But what she didn't know was what had become obvious to me and everyone else. She was my miracle. And I needed no other. With her I was enriched.

Author's Note

Hi there, friends!

So there you have it! The real story of the Holy Grail (aka the sacred chalice)! I hope you enjoyed my retelling of the quest for this ancient relic.

As with all my medieval stories, I included a fantasy element but also tried to keep it grounded in reality, so that hopefully by the end, you are left wondering (like the characters) whether what happened was a miracle or a result of natural means. Was the jotunn really a troll or simply a deranged madman? Could he give out curses or was the bleeding a result of genetics? Did the chalice heal, or did Karina's love bring about the miracle?

Regardless of whether you liked the fantasy elements, I hope you adored the love story between Karina and Torvald. I always enjoy writing arranged marriage stories! And this one was really fun because both characters were such complete opposites.

So, what's coming next, you might be asking? Well, of course, Espen and Kristoffer need their happily-ever-afters! But how will they find true love with war and danger so imminent? I hope you'll stay tuned for the final two books coming soon.

If you want to find out more about the other books in this series, please visit my website at jodyhedlund.com or check out my Facebook Reader Room, where I chat with readers and post news about my books.

Until next time . . .

Jody Hedlund is the best-selling author of over thirty historicals for both adults and teens and is the winner of numerous awards including the Christy, Carol, and Christian Book Award. She lives in central Michigan with her husband, busy family, and five spoiled cats. Learn more at jodyhedlund.com.

More Young Adult Fiction from Jody Hedlund
Knights of Brethren

Enamored

Having been raised by her childless aunt and uncle, the king and queen, Princess Elinor finds herself the only heir to the throne of Norvegia. As she comes of age, she must choose a husband to rule beside her, but she struggles to make her selection from among a dozen noblemen during a weeklong courtship.

Entwined

After growing up on a remote farm, Lis learns she is the rightful heir to the throne of Norvegia. Even as she does her part to thwart a dangerous plot against the king, she resists pursuing her new identity and resigns herself to a simple life helping her elderly father with their farm.

Ensnared

Nursemaid to the Earl of Likness's two young daughters, Mikaela despises the earl for his cruelty to his subjects, and she longs for the day when she can make a difference in the lives of her suffering friends and family.

Enriched

Lady Karina lives in a convent and expects to become a nun someday. When her wealthy father asks her to help his textile business become more successful by marrying one of the popular Knights of Brethren, Karina complies, ever the dutiful daughter.

The Fairest Maidens

Beholden

Upon the death of her wealthy father, Lady Gabriella is condemned to work in Warwick's gem mine. As she struggles to survive the dangerous conditions, her kindness and beauty shine as brightly as the jewels the slaves excavate. While laboring, Gabriella plots how to avenge her father's death and stop Queen Margery's cruelty.

Beguiled

Princess Pearl flees for her life after her mother, Queen Margery, tries to have her killed during a hunting expedition. Pearl finds refuge on the Isle of Outcasts among criminals and misfits, disguising her face with a veil so no one recognizes her. She lives for the day when she can return to Warwick and rescue her sister, Ruby, from the queen's clutches.

Besotted

Queen Aurora of Mercia has spent her entire life deep in Inglewood Forest, hiding from Warwick's Queen Margery, who seeks her demise. As the time draws near for Aurora to take the throne, she happens upon a handsome woodcutter. Although friendship with outsiders is forbidden and dangerous, she cannot stay away from the charming stranger.

The Lost Princesses

Always: Prequel Novella

On the verge of dying after giving birth to twins, the queen of Mercia pleads with Lady Felicia to save her infant daughters. With the castle overrun by King Ethelwulf's invading army, Lady Felicia vows to do whatever she can to take the newborn princesses and their three-year-old sister to safety, even though it means sacrificing everything she holds dear, possibly her own life.

Evermore

Raised by a noble family, Lady Adelaide has always known she's an orphan. Little does she realize she's one of the lost princesses and the true heir to Mercia's throne . . . until a visitor arrives at her family estate, reveals her birthright as queen, and thrusts her into a quest for the throne whether she's ready or not.

Foremost

Raised in an isolated abbey, Lady Maribel desires nothing more than to become a nun and continue practicing her healing arts. She's carefree and happy with her life . . . until a visitor comes to the abbey and reveals her true identity as one of the lost princesses.

Hereafter

Forced into marriage, Emmeline has one goal—to escape. But Ethelrex takes his marriage vows seriously, including his promise to love and cherish his wife, and he has no intention of letting Emmeline get away. As the battle for the throne rages, will the prince be able to win the battle for Emmeline's heart?

The Noble Knights

The Vow

Young Rosemarie finds herself drawn to Thomas, the son of the nearby baron. But just as her feelings begin to grow, a man carrying the Plague interrupts their hunting party. While in forced isolation, Rosemarie begins to contemplate her future—could it include Thomas? Could he be the perfect man to one day rule beside her and oversee her parents' lands?

An Uncertain Choice

Due to her parents' promise at her birth, Lady Rosemarie has been prepared to become a nun on the day she turns eighteen. Then, shortly before her birthday, a friend of her father's enters the kingdom and proclaims her parents' will left a second choice—if Rosemarie can marry before the eve of her eighteenth year, she will be exempt from the ancient vow.

A Daring Sacrifice

In a reverse twist on the Robin Hood story, a young medieval maiden stands up for the rights of the mistreated, stealing from the rich to give to the poor. All the while, she fights against her cruel uncle who has taken over the land that is rightfully hers.

For Love & Honor

Lady Sabine is harboring a skin blemish, one that if revealed could cause her to be branded as a witch, put her life in danger, and damage her chances of making a good marriage. After all, what nobleman would want to marry a woman so flawed?

A Loyal Heart

When Lady Olivia's castle is besieged, she and her sister are taken captive and held for ransom by her father's enemy, Lord Pitt. Loyalty to family means everything to Olivia. She'll save her sister at any cost and do whatever her father asks—even if that means obeying his order to steal a sacred relic from her captor.

A Worthy Rebel

While fleeing an arranged betrothal to a heartless lord, Lady Isabelle becomes injured and lost. Rescued by a young peasant man, she hides her identity as a noblewoman for fear of reprisal from the peasants who are bitter and angry toward the nobility.

A complete list of my novels can be found at jodyhedlund.com.

Would you like to know when my next book is available? You can sign up for my newsletter, become my friend on Goodreads, like me on Facebook, or follow me on Twitter.

Newsletter: jodyhedlund.com
Goodreads:
goodreads.com/author/show/3358829.Jody_Hedlund
Facebook: facebook.com/AuthorJodyHedlund
Twitter: @JodyHedlund

The more reviews a book has, the more likely other readers are to find it. If you have a minute, please leave a rating or review. I appreciate all reviews, whether positive or negative.